THE CAPE MAY GARDEN

CLAUDIA VANCE

CHAPTER ONE

Spring hadn't lasted long this year. Hot days arrived way too quickly. It was another year where winter felt like it rolled right into summer, practically skipping spring altogether. This wasn't ideal for growing cold-weather crops like the lettuce and spinach that Margaret had in the ground. She needed to start getting her summer vegetable garden planted, especially since she had things she wanted to get off her mind—like Paul, her husband of fifteen years who'd abruptly walked out a month ago, leaving nothing but a note on the kitchen counter.

I'm sorry. I need a break.

"That was it. That was all the note said. No call. No text. No discussion. No goodbye. He just left. He never came home from work one day. Turned his phone off too," Margaret practically shouted into the phone as she tried to one-handedly hoe the garden.

"I can't believe it!" said Sarah, her best friend since fourth grade. "I thought I knew him. I'm honestly shocked. I never thought in a million years he would do that."

Margaret sighed. "You're telling me. It was quite a shock, and the girls are still clueless. I had to tell our daughters that Dad was on an impromptu work trip. They are starting to get suspicious since it's been a month already, though … Well, let me call you later, trying to hoe this garden with one hand is *not* working."

Sarah sighed. "OK, but please call me when you have time. We need to discuss this."

Even though it had already been a month since Paul left, Margaret had just started telling those closest to her, aside from her mother. She'd needed time to process everything first. After all, she wasn't quite sure what was happening herself. At first, she thought that he'd be back in a day or so, then days turned into weeks, and then, an entire month had gone by.

It was already 82 degrees out, and sweat poured off of Margaret's face as she prepared her soil. It was her favorite day of the year—planting day. It was a day of sunblock from head to toe, lots of ice-cold lemon water, big wide brim hats and dirt everywhere.

It was absolutely, positively a wonderful day for Margaret. Nothing could ruin her most cherished day of the year. It had been this way since she was a little girl helping her grandfather in his massive garden. Planting day was a tradition. It was marked on the calendar. Her husband's desertion wasn't going to stop her this year.

She added fresh compost to her garden plots from her compost bin and got all of her seeds in order. It was mid-May, prime time in New Jersey to get her crops in the ground. She started all of her heirloom seeds inside under grow lights and had lots of them to plant. She was probably going to be out in this sun for hours, but she didn't care one bit. She was ready to soak in all that vitamin D.

"Ew, why are there so many worms everywhere?!" shrieked Abby, Margaret's six-year-old daughter.

"I think they're cool!" replied Harper, Margaret's eight-year-old, while studying a long earthworm she dangled above her head.

Margaret's two daughters were exact opposites. Abby was

afraid of everything including her own shadow, while Harper liked to find and pick up harmless snakes outside for fun. If she was feeling super naughty, she'd chase her sister around with one.

Margaret wiped the sweat off her brow with the back of her hand and motioned for the girls to come over. "Alright, you two! Are you helping me today or what? So far, you only seem interested in looking at the worms."

Abby and Harper stopped what they were doing and skipped over. Abby was in a sundress and sandals and Harper in overalls, rain boots, and a backwards hat. One was dressed for helping Mom in the garden, and the other just thought she was.

Margaret looked the two up and down and chuckled. "How about you two start planting some bean seeds in the rows I've already hoed? You remember what I taught you about how to space them apart, right?"

Both girls nodded and raced to the seed packets, each hoping to pick their favorite before the other.

"I want to plant the purple beans!" yelled Abby as she ran.

"Remember to mark the rows with what you planted. Otherwise, we'll never remember!" Margaret hollered out as they feverishly looked through the seeds.

Margaret knew the risks of having children plant seeds. It meant probably having too many seeds planted in one spot, or them forgetting what they planted before there was time to mark it. Margaret didn't mind, though. She wanted her children to feel the awe and wonder of the garden like she had as a child with her grandfather. Plus, she knew she could always thin the seedlings out once they sprouted. And the mystery of figuring out what the unmarked plants were as they grew was actually kind of fun. The girls enjoyed helping, and she enjoyed having them out there with her.

* * *

Margaret was a 45-year-old workhorse . She was always tackling a new project, whether it was refurbishing a piece of furniture she'd thrifted, sewing a dress, cooking the most scrumptious food, or randomly putting in new tile and paint in the bathroom. Completely self-taught, of course.

Her top choice of projects was gardening though. There was just something special about planting a super tiny seed in the ground and watching it grow and flourish every day. Tomatoes were her preferred thing to grow, and she looked forward to making fresh tomato and mayonnaise sandwiches every summer.

You could always catch her traveling; she enjoyed the beach, hiking, and camping. She involved the girls in most of what she did. Paul would sometimes go, but you could tell it wasn't always his idea of fun. He was more of a homebody who enjoyed routine. He was the complete opposite of Margaret and her spontaneity, but they somehow made it work. That is, until now.

When Margaret wasn't gardening or doing the other things she loved to do, she was managing a nonprofit wildlife rescue hospital. It was located on a wildlife refuge called Pine Tree Wildlife Refuge a few towns over. Spring and summer were especially busy, and that meant an influx of orphaned fauna that had to be cared for. Despite the (sometimes) long hours and dirty work, she loved her job, her coworkers, and the many dedicated volunteers who showed up daily to help.

* * *

"I'm not sure if I feel lonely, sad, indifferent, or what. I mean, Paul and I never fought. It's not like we hated each other. It's just weird. Yeah, we had our problems, but I never thought *this* would happen," Margaret said to Sarah as they ate lunch on the patio.

Sarah nodded. "I totally understand. It's strange. Are you

supposed to move on? I mean, how long is he away for? Do you even *want* to be with him when he comes back? There are a lot of unanswered questions here."

Margaret sighed. "Yeah, it's all so confusing. I'm really upset about the girls the most though. Not sure how you can be gone a month and not even care to talk to or see your daughters."

Sarah looked at her hands and nodded in agreement. "Yep. It just doesn't make sense."

As Margaret sat with her oldest friend, she admired her beloved backyard. Not only did she treasure growing vegetables and herbs, but she was fond of flowers as well. Her yard was something out of a magazine. Full of large trees, beautiful lilac blooms, lush greenery, whimsical wind chimes, and chirping birds, it evoked a magical quality. Well-manicured green hedges lined the many maze-like walkways leading to different secret gardens and resting spots with various birdbaths and feeders and lots of shady little reading nooks tucked away in the corners.

Margaret's house was "down the shore" in Cape May, as those in New Jersey called it. West Cape May, to be exact. The beach was a mere quarter mile away. It was a smaller property nestled amongst a winery, other residences, and some horse farms. Not too far in the opposite direction were marshlands full of shore birds and the lighthouse.

Margaret had prepared a homemade egg salad recipe from eggs out of her chicken coop.

"You have to add the diced pickles in this egg salad. It makes it," Margaret said as she took a bite.

On the table was lavender lemonade (her secret recipe) and some chips (made from scratch) that she had whipped up earlier that day. Margaret had many skills, including cooking some of the best things her guests had ever tasted on the fly out of random items in her pantry and garden.

Sarah mumbled through her bites how good everything

was. "This is truly excellent, Margaret. I think you're onto something here."

* * *

"These showed up after we had a tree cut down," said a man with a look of concern on his face, while holding a box at the counter of the wildlife hospital. Inside was a towel with a pile of sleeping orphaned squirrels. Margaret felt tenderness for the little critters, who were all snuggled together trying to keep warm.

She had the man fill out a form and gently took the box to the intake room for the volunteers to handle. This was of normal occurrence lately; it was baby season after all.

They had all sorts of animals in their care: raccoons, foxes, deer, birds, ducks, chipmunks, bunnies, opossums. The volunteers and workers that Margaret managed knew exactly what to do with the baby squirrels. It made Margaret's life a lot easier having a good staff that she could count on. This job could get overwhelming this time of the year.

A wildlife refuge worker named Dave, who lived on the premises, had been working there for years, even longer than Margaret, though he had just started living there a year ago. The wildlife hospital sat on many acres of land deep in the forest, and Dave was in charge of building enclosures for animals that couldn't be released into the wild, whether due to a broken wing that couldn't be fixed, or they had too much of a human imprint on them, or other such reasons. Dave seemed a bit of a mystery to her.

While Margaret was filling out the paperwork for the newest squirrels, Dave walked in, sweaty and dirty from lugging lumber and ladders around.

"Do you need anything in here? I'm going to the store for some things."

Margaret looked around to see what may be in short supply. "Maybe some paper towels?"

Before she knew it, the swinging door slammed shut and Dave was gone. *Sheesh, he was in a hurry.*

Dave was a hard nut to crack. They rarely talked because he was always busy outside building things, and Margaret was always tending to animals inside. When they did talk, he never discussed his personal life, and he always seemed to be at the refuge lately. She wondered if he had a life outside of it.

It was a little after 9 p.m. when Margaret locked up for the night. Now that it was warmer out, they changed to later hours to keep all the wildlife babies fed into the evening and to allow people more time to bring in orphaned or injured wildlife.

The refuge was gorgeous with tall pine trees and the full moon reflecting off the nearby lake. The smell of campfire filled the air, making Margaret nostalgic for the family camping trips she enjoyed as a kid in the Pine Barrens.

Usually, Margaret used a flashlight on the way to her car in the complete darkness, but the moon definitely helped light her path tonight as the low sounds of chirping peeper frogs filled the serene air.

* * *

"Ow! Ew!" This was definitely the downside to being a nature girl and working at a wildlife refuge. Margaret didn't flinch when it came to snakes or spiders, but a tick was her worst enemy, and finding one on her person so early in the day was not her idea of a good morning. Successfully removing the little blood sucker, her phone rang just as she was washing up..

"You *are not* going to believe this!" said Liz, her younger sister.

"Uh, OK, tell me … and don't leave out any of the dirty details."

"We just bought a beach house on acres of land down the

road from you. It's right near Sunset Beach. We were thinking about fixing it up and flipping it, but a part of us is dreaming of what it would be like to live there, and I think we're going to do it. We're moving in this weekend."

Margaret was in disbelief. "Wait. As in two days? How on earth are you going to pull that off so quickly?"

"Yep. The owners have already moved to North Carolina, so everything was moved out. They accepted our offer, and voila! We've been in escrow over a month ago, but we just didn't tell anyone. We could have taken our time and fixed the place up before moving in, but we're too excited to wait! Of course, we still have to sell our current place, but I'm pretty sure it will sell fast since the neighborhood is so coveted. We just had to jump on this chance."

Liz was the sister who'd always had big dreams and aspirations in life. She constantly incorporated change. She and Greg had lived in the city for a long while, and then the 'burbs, right over the bridge from the city. Now they were moving to the beach and would be a lot closer to both Margaret and their parents with this new venture.

Liz and Greg's kids were in middle school and had very busy lives, much busier than Margaret's, in fact. Each kid played three sports, had a zillion friends with a corresponding number of birthday parties to attend, were in multiple clubs, and always had homework. It was hard to figure out how they had time to sleep.

Margaret was excited by the thought of having her sister's family move closer—especially for her girls, they loved their cousins. This could mean more impromptu porch hangouts and fun drop-in Sunday dinners.

* * *

The next morning, Margaret had some time to garden before she had to make her way to work. She took a deep breath as she walked through the archway full of climbing roses that led to her vegetable garden. The sun was starting to rise, and there was a thick fog that laid close to the ground.

She always enjoyed being out here, but morning was her favorite time. It wasn't too hot yet, and still peaceful and quiet.

Walking around barefoot connected her to the earth. It was her time to focus on herself and be with nature. To have serenity before the rest of the world around her woke up. It was her own meditation.

After about an hour out in the garden, Margaret went back into the house to rouse the girls, make them breakfast, and get them off to school. There was still another month of school until summer break.

"Rise and shine, my little sunshines!" Margaret lilted as she opened the blinds to let the golden rays pour in to wake her daughters up.

Abby and Harper shared a room by choice. As polar opposite as they were, they still enjoyed each other's company. Margaret also suspected they were both afraid of the dark and felt safer together.

"Ugh, Mom! Do I have to go?" Harper said as she slowly pulled herself up to sitting.

Abby jumped out of bed, threw a dress on, and quickly dragged a comb through her hair. "Mom, why hasn't Dad called? He usually calls when he travels for work. It feels like it's been a long time since we've talked to him."

Margaret was caught off guard by the question. She felt horrible for lying about the situation to them, but she also felt they wouldn't understand the truth and would be more hurt by it. Frankly, even the adults couldn't understand the truth. How would a child?

Margaret redirected, "Well, I'm not quite sure, honey. He's probably super busy at work. Anyway, let's get you ready for school. We have thirty minutes to get ready and eat breakfast before we hop in the car."

After dropping the girls off at school, Margaret drove to work. It was roughly a twenty-minute drive with traffic. As she pulled in, she noticed Dave sitting at the picnic table sipping a coffee. She'd never seen him sitting. Ever. The man was always moving.

"Good morning, Dave," Margaret said on her way in.

Dave lifted his coffee mug, smiled, and nodded. "Morning, Margaret."

Margaret waved and kept walking. A part of her never realized how attractive Dave was, in his own way. He had these dirty, beat-up hands from working with them all day, but they looked strong and steady, especially around that coffee cup. Margaret giggled to herself at the thought.

He had piercing blue eyes, and his brawny arms fit tightly in his short-sleeved shirt. He had tan skin, presumably from being outside at his job all day, and thick, wavy salt-and-pepper hair that he pushed behind his ears constantly to keep out of his eyes. He definitely had a simultaneous rustic lumberjack and surfer dude vibe.

For some reason, that day Margaret had decided to dress up a little for work, which she never did since it usually was such a dirty job. She'd let her long brown hair down for once instead of keeping it in a tight bun, had a tiny bit of makeup on that still let her freckles peek through, and wore a fitted gray short-sleeved shirt under new floral overalls. She felt pretty.

She also felt eyes on her after she walked past Dave.

Margaret instantly felt guilty for even thinking about attraction right now while she was going through this confusing mess with her husband. Nothing was set in stone yet. She didn't know what was going to happen. She needed to get her mind out of the gutter for now.

Or did she?

CHAPTER TWO

Abby and Harper were getting ready for school when the house phone suddenly rang. They raced to the phone like their lives depended on it.

Harper managed to get to the phone first. "Hello." The line was silent. "Hello?!"

The line was still silent.

"Here. Give me *that*!" Abby said as she tore the phone away from her sister. "Hello? Dad?? Is that you?"

There was a click and the person on the other end hung up.

Abby slammed the phone down and ran upstairs, hysterically crying. Harper just shrugged her shoulders.

"Mom," Harper yelled out.

"Yes, honey?" Margaret answered from the upstairs bathroom where she was getting ready for work.

"Abby is upset about Dad. Someone called the house just now and she thought it was him."

"I'll take care of it, Harp. Just finish eating and getting ready so we can leave." Margaret was starting to feel very angry with Paul for causing this mess, but she didn't have time for anger right then. Her daughters needed her and she had a schedule to keep.

Both girls were really starting to be affected by their father's sudden departure and subsequent silence, but especially Abby. She was the closest to him. She was a daddy's girl. They were two peas in a pod.

* * *

That evening while leaving work, Margaret grabbed her ringing cell phone from the bottom of her bag.

"Hi, Mom. What's up?" She hoped nothing was wrong. Judy watched the girls on the evenings she needed to work late, and it was unlike her to call.

"Hey, Margaret. Everything is fine here, but I happened to overhear a message being left on the house phone's answering machine. Abby's teacher wants you to call her. Is everything alright?"

"Thanks, Mom. I'm not sure. Abby has been acting weird since Paul left, and I have a feeling it has affected her in school. I guess we'll find out."

Margaret had noticed that Abby, the normally studious one, didn't seem to care about school anymore. Instead of doing her homework on her own before dinner, Margaret had to keep after her, and the nagging turned into fights. She had lost complete interest in anything school related. That negative perspective was *not* Abby.

When Margaret got home, she scarfed down some leftovers from the dinner her mother had made for the girls and quickly called Abby's teacher back.

"Hi, Mrs. Kunkle? This is Margaret Wilder, Abby's mom, returning your call."

"Hi, Margaret. Thank you so much for calling me back. I wanted to talk to you about some concerns I have with Abby. Over the past few weeks, I've seen a big change in her attitude and performance at school. She is normally one of the brightest and most engaged students in the classroom, but lately she's been acting out some and has not been doing that great on tests. I was wondering if maybe something was happening at home that could be causing this?"

"Mrs. Kunkle, I appreciate you alerting me of this. Her father and I have been having some issues and are sort of separated at the moment, and I definitely feel like it's affected her. I will have a talk with her. Thank you."

Margaret swallowed hard after she hung up. Suddenly she felt sick. She had no idea how she was going to talk to Abby about all of this without upsetting her and making it worse.

* * *

The next day was Margaret's day off, and she was itching to see Liz and Greg's new house down the road. Once the girls were in school, Margaret made her way over.

Pulling down a long winding driveway, bordered on either side by unkept meadows filled with colorful wildflowers in shades of yellow, white, and purple, she found herself already impressed with this place. When she finally reached the end of the driveway, which felt like a five-minute drive from the street, an old purple Victorian house came into view. It had a porch that wrapped around the side of the house, complete with rocking chairs and colorful patterned pillows and ferns that hung from hooks every two feet. Chickens walked around, grazing freely, and Liz and Greg's two dogs ran out the front door to greet her on the steps almost immediately.

Liz was an interior designer and it showed. They'd just moved in and already the porch looked like it was straight out of magazine.

On top of being an amazing interior designer, she was a master at thrifty economics, specializing in restoring run-down pieces to show their beauty. She was constantly picking discarded furniture off of curbs and scouring thrift stores to find projects for herself. The two sisters were very much alike in that sense.

"Well, it's about time you came over. We could've used your help moving the million boxes and furniture in," Liz said, half-jokingly. Liz was not one to hold back what she was thinking. Ever.

"I know. The Pine Tree Wildlife Refuge Hospital is now open four extra hours, and it's busy season with all the orphaned babies. So sorry I wasn't able to carry all this on my back for you," joked Margaret.

Neither sister had a filter. If one said something sarcastic, the other just shot back with something even more sarcastic or inappropriate. It was a bit of a game they'd played since they were kids.

"Do you like the chickens that the previous owners left behind for us? We have no idea what to do with them. You have to help us, that's your area of expertise."

"I would love to. I have all the time in the world," Margaret joked.

"Well, get on in here already. I have to show you around!" Liz said excitedly.

Margaret paused on the porch and marveled at the oak entry doors with beveled glass panels. "Mom and Dad will love this. They may ask to move in."

Margaret and Liz's parents were some of the best parents around. They gave Liz and Margaret such amazingly fun and memorable childhoods and supported them in everything they did, and now they all lived within a half hour of each other. It was perfect.

Margaret and Liz grew up with a lot to live up to in terms of romance because their parents were the most in love couple they knew. Forty-seven years of marriage and they still held hands all of the time and still preferred a queen bed over a king because they could be closer to each other when they slept.

The story of how their parents met was something that both Margaret and Liz loved to share with people.

It was the summer of 1970.

They were nineteen-year-olds on the Wildwood Boardwalk along the South Jersey coastline. Margaret's mom, Judy, was working the ice cream stand and their dad, Bob, was walking with a group of friends when he looked over and saw the girl of his dreams in a white uniform wearing a paper hat and scooping ice cream.

Well, he told his friends that he would catch up with them, and to keep on going. He got in line at the ice cream stand and asked Judy for a vanilla cone and a date. Judy blushed and declined.

However, an hour later, Bob came back with his friends and got down on his knees in the middle of the very busy boardwalk and sang his heart out to her. He even had his friends get in on the singing. The whole boardwalk came to a standstill around them and watched.

At the end of the song, he stood up and said, "I don't know your name. I don't know where you live. I don't know anything about you, but will you take a chance and please go on a date with me? Because you are the most beautiful girl in the whole wide world, and I'd love to get to know you."

When he was done, everyone on the boardwalk clapped and chanted, "Go on a date! Go on a date!" At that point, Judy's coworkers were giddy and screaming and jumping up and down because they could only wish that something this romantic would happen to them someday.

Judy accepted, and that very night, Bob met Judy after her shift ended on the boardwalk. They spent hours talking and walking while getting to know each other amongst the bright neon lights of the stores, the loud screams and *whooshes* coming from the roller coasters, and the cool ocean breeze in their hair. They were married three years later, and the rest is history.

* * *

Margaret adored every second of the tour of Liz and Greg's house. It was built a lot like her home. In fact, Margaret's current house used to be their childhood home. Margaret bought it from her parents before she met Paul. She'd always been a hard worker and a saver, starting at a young age. She played it smart, and couldn't bear to see her childhood home go to someone outside the family when her parents decided to move.

"So, I was thinking of making this room the family room instead of the dining room because it's bigger than the family room and has more windows," Liz said as she zipped through the house.

"And this kitchen. Phew! We are tearing down these walls and this wall, adding an island, and putting in new flooring. I also want a double-sided farm sink." Liz sighed and paused. "Actually, pretty much gutting and redoing it entirely. But wait until you see the yard. You are going to flip out!"

Margaret could barely get a word in because Liz was so excited and had so much to say.

Liz had always wanted to move back to the beach. This was where they'd grown up, after all, and her family and most of her longtime friends were still in the area. This always felt truly like home to her, no matter where she lived or how cozy she decorated the space.

She'd worked for years to persuade Greg, but he hadn't seriously entertained it because the long commute to his job wasn't feasible. However, Greg was now able to work from home, so it all worked out.

Liz ran past Greg, who was putting together furniture, and grabbed her sister's arm. "OK, watch your step. We still have to get these back steps fixed. Now, close your eyes and take my hand. I've got a surprise."

"Hi, Greg. Bye, Greg," Margaret joked as she was led past her brother-in-law.

The sun was just starting to set, and Margaret felt like she'd walked for an eternity to wherever Liz was taking her.

"Um, OK. Are you taking me into the woods to off me or what? We've been walking forever," Margaret half-joked.

Liz stopped. "OK, open your eyes!"

On the other side of the property, along the road, was a little farm stand. Beat up, dingy, mostly rotted, and barely seen through all the overgrowth. Still, there stood what she could imagine was a once-cute farm stand, nonetheless.

"This is yours?" Margaret asked, astonished.

"Yes. It came with this house. All of this property is ours. I've been finding new treasures every day here. This land used to be a working farm years ago, and this farm stand hasn't been used since. It's completely run-down."

Margaret felt her heart flutter with excitement for a second. She'd always had a dream of starting a side business selling what she grew and cooked up, even if just for a little extra vacation money. Her nonprofit job paid the bills, but it didn't make her rich by any means.

Suddenly, Margaret's excitement turned sour, changing to uncertainty. She remembered she hadn't told Liz yet about Paul leaving. She'd only told Sarah and her mother.

"Look, Liz, since I have you alone right now, I need to tell you something," Margaret said, looking off into the distance.

"Oh, you mean about Paul leaving a month ago?" Liz blurted out.

"Who told you?" Margaret was now annoyed.

"Mom did. I wasn't supposed to tell you I knew, but since you were about to tell me, I figured I'd beat you to the punch," Liz said with a half-smirk.

Liz and Margaret were super close with their mom. The

three of them had turned into true friends, meeting up for brunch or dinner dates regularly. It made sense that their mom couldn't keep that big a secret.

Liz and Margaret's relationship with their mother hadn't always been great though. They were once angsty teenagers who stayed out past curfew, dated "bad boys," and rebelled every chance they got.

They'd engaged in a good number of arguments with their mother during high school. In fact, it got really bad Margaret's junior year. At one point, she'd been sent to live with their great aunt Mary in Delaware for the summer. By the time they went to college, they had matured, made better decisions, and everything turned out for the best. Margaret hoped it never got that way with her daughters.

Liz was only a year younger than Margaret, so growing up they were always close. They had the same circle of friends and while Margaret was more popular than Liz, she always included her in everything she did, which explained why Liz was dragged into Margaret's rebellious phase.

"So, how are you doing? I couldn't say anything for the past month and it was killing me. I can't believe you didn't tell me," Liz said, intently staring at her sister.

"I'm doing OK. In fact, it's been making me reevaluate a lot in terms of what I want. However, the girls aren't doing so well with it, and I'm beyond angry at him right now for upsetting them." She couldn't help that her hands clenched of their own accord.

"We have been together since I was twenty-five. Five years of dating, fifteen years of marriage … we may look like the perfect couple, we really aren't. We're very different, and as the years go on, we're growing more and more different from each other. Now this …"

Liz cut in. "Yeah, I've noticed that but never felt comfortable saying anything. You love to travel and he doesn't. You've always traveled with friends and family—even by yourself.

Don't you want someone you can do all that with? I get that you don't need *all* the same hobbies and interests, but traveling is kind of a special thing to experience with someone, no?"

Margaret sighed. "Well, I actually do love traveling solo and with friends ... but yeah, it would be nice to have a significant other to experience the joy of traveling with at times."

Before Margaret could get another word out, Liz went on another rant. "And don't get me started on the gardening. That man has never mowed the lawn, raked a leaf, or planted a seed. Does he even cook with what you grow?"

Liz was right. Margaret loved traveling and the outdoors and Paul hated it. They were completely different. *How had it worked for as long as it had?*

"Yeah, I'm not sure what to do until I can talk to him again. Abby is doing badly in school right now because of all of this, and it's extremely upsetting. I'm thinking about having her talk to a counselor at school, or outside of school. Maybe both Harper and Abby should talk to someone."

Liz nodded. "Well, we're right around the corner for you and the girls now. The boys too. They're actually probably getting done with soccer practice pretty soon and I have to pick them up. Good thing I remembered or they'd be hitchhiking," Liz joked.

Though the sun had completely set, the sky still had pink streaks left. "Look, let's get back to the house before it's dark. I didn't bring a flashlight and it will be pitch-black out here before we know it," Liz said.

As they walked back to the house, Margaret admired the land Liz and Greg now lived on. It was way bigger than Margaret's property. She daydreamed about what the farm and farm stand used to be like.

"So, this old beat-up farm stand and all of this land ... What are you thinking, Liz?" Margaret asked with curiosity and a hint of excitement.

Liz smiled. "Sister, I want you to decide that. I look at it and I see you. Greg and I both see you. The boys even said it makes them think of you. Maybe we can dig up some history and do research on what this property used to be like."

Liz turned towards the thick tree line on the property. "I forgot to tell you, all that forest area back there is ours too. I walked back there with the boys yesterday and there are a ton of old hidden, overgrown chicken coops that look like they haven't been touched in twenty years. I found a super old glass bottle in one. It actually feels like a treasure hunt exploring this property. I wonder what other abandoned things are hidden here?"

"This is absolutely amazing," Margaret said as she stopped to look back at the purple sky full of fireflies, Mother Nature's version of twinkle lights.

Margaret felt full of happiness in this moment. Not just because there could be some great potential on this land, but because her thoughtful family had her in mind when they bought the place. For a minute, she even forgot about her husband leaving.

CHAPTER THREE

The next morning, Margaret received a phone call an hour before she was due at work. It was her supervisor, Joan. This was somewhat odd because Joan never called her; they pretty much only corresponded in person at work or through work e-mail.

Margaret awkwardly answered her cell phone. "Hello?"

"Hey, Margaret, it's Joan."

"Hi, Joan. What's up?"

Joan paused. "Well, I guess I'm going to come right out with it. I don't have good news, Margaret. Our donations have been on a decline for the past few years, and this year is the worst we've seen it. Being a nonprofit, you know we are very dependent on donations and our volunteers to keep the wildlife rehabilitation hospital and grounds running. In order to stay open, we have to make some cutbacks. I'm so sorry. We are only going to be able to pay you for part-time hours, so your hours will be cut in half starting next week. We foresee this being temporary until we can figure out how to improve our donations. We are going to have the lead volunteer, Janice, be there on the days you won't be. This is what we have to do to make sure the hospital stays afloat during this hard time."

Margaret couldn't believe it. They hadn't ever needed to cut employee hours in all the years she'd worked there. It was hard not to take it personally at first, thinking about how she'd worked her way up to hospital manager. All the blood, sweat, and tears, not to mention overtime, were undertaken with gusto. Deep down she understood though. She knew how much the refuge depended on donations. But why had the donations dropped so much? What had changed?

What horrible timing this all was. Paul leaving, the girls having issues, and now work hours were cut in *half*.

Was Mercury in retrograde? What in the world was going on? Why was everything crashing at her feet?

Margaret hung up the phone and did the first thing that came to mind, which was to call her mother.

"Hello, it's a beautiful day down the shore!" Judy answered with the most cheerful enthusiasm on the planet.

"Mom. I'm glad it's beautiful, but uh … I just got my hours cut in half. Donations are down significantly for the first time in years, and they had to make some temporary cutbacks."

"Oh no! Are you going to be OK financially with everything going on?" Judy's cheerfulness vanished.

"Well, I might be able to get partial unemployment, but I still may make too much a week with part-time hours to qualify. With whatever is going on with Paul, and now work, this is all super stressful."

"Well, you know your father and I are always here for anything you need."

"I know, Mom. Thank you. OK, let me go. I have to get to work."

Margaret hung up the phone and finished getting ready, all the while wondering who else had their hours reduced.

* * *

When Margaret got to work, Dave wasn't at the picnic table, which—oddly—made her feel a little bummed. She was hoping to maybe ask him if he'd had his hours cut back too.

She was working with all volunteers today, so there wasn't anyone to commiserate with unless she called or went to talk to those in the education department in the other building.

The hospital was busy the entire day, and Margaret didn't see Dave once. Usually, she would see him once or twice, even if he was just walking by one of the windows.

Everything felt weird, and suddenly Margaret had a sense of fear. What if this situation really hurt her financially? What would she do? What if *temporary* meant many months or even a year? Paul wasn't around to discuss this with.

It was dark out when Margaret finished her shift and raced to her car. She needed to get out of there. The stress from the cutback had built over the course of the day. She immediately called Sarah. She needed to talk to someone. She had to vent. She had to clear her mind. She had to dish her fears. Who better to listen than her best friend?

"Hey, Margaret. Whatcha doing?"

"Oh, you know, just leaving my job that *cut my hours in half,*" Margaret blurted out.

"Oh no! Why?"

"It's a nonprofit and they have to cut corners while they improve donations. It is what it is, but I'm a little worried about finances. We can discuss later. Say, are you free to come over for some snacks and drinks? I really need a gab session to clear my mind. Today has been entirely awful."

"Yes, I can be over in an hour."

In the meantime, Margaret felt the urge to talk with her girls about what was going on. She didn't like lying to them. They were old enough to know something was wrong. It was affecting them, after all. Especially Abby and her schoolwork.

After Judy left the house, Margaret had to figure out what

to say. No, she wasn't going to lie anymore. The truth. That's what she was going to stick with.

"How are my girls?" Margaret asked as the girls sat on the couch watching TV.

Too consumed with their show, they both just shrugged and mumbled something in response.

"I feel like we need to talk," Margaret said, using the remote to turn off the television.

Now she had annoyed both of them.

"I want to talk about your father."

They both perked up and looked straight at her. *Now* she had their attention.

"Yes, Mom. We would like some answers," Abby bluntly said back.

"The reason your dad hasn't called while he's away is a mystery to me. He's not away for work. I only said that because I don't know where he is. He went somewhere and turned off his phone. I think he needed time alone, just like when you girls sometimes need time by yourselves. I think Daddy has things he has to work out with himself. He loves you, and just know this isn't because of anything you have done."

Abby started crying.

Margaret hugged her and pushed her hair softly off her face.

"Abby, I don't want you to worry or stress. Please don't let this affect your schoolwork."

Margaret had no clue if she was doing this right. Was it appropriate to have told the truth? Had she been too blunt? Should she have left some things out? How can any parent be prepared for this?

Seemingly unfazed, Harper looked straight into her mother's eyes. Margaret awaited what was to happen next.

"OK, thank you for the truth. Can I have the remote back, please?"

Margaret was taken aback by this. Harper had just found

out their father purposely left without calling for a month and all she cared about was the remote?

"Sure," Margaret said, tossing it to her. "Don't you want to discuss Dad? Don't you have questions, Harp?"

"I mean, not really. I think he'll be back. I've seen this kind of thing happen on TV. People sometimes need breaks to find themselves again. He's probably having a midlife crisis or something. You know, whatever that doctor guy on TV talks about."

Margaret had no clue what kind of TV show Harper was talking about, but she seemed to have some sort understanding of what may have been happening.

"Well, Aunt Sarah is coming over to hang out in bit, but I want you girls to go get ready for bed. You can stay up until ten reading your books, but that's it. You need your sleep for school."

Twenty minutes later, there was a knock at the back door. "Come in!" Margaret said while slicing some cheese and apples in the kitchen.

"Hey!"

"Hi."

Margaret registered hearing two voices not one at the same time Sarah and Liz walked in.

"OK, I felt like we really needed a girl gab session, and I happened to be talking to your sister before I came over, and I thought she should come, too. The more the merrier?" Sarah said as she popped a piece of cheese into her mouth before turning to open the fridge. Presumably to look for wine.

"Yes, sister, I can't believe I didn't get an invite," Liz half-joked as she held a homemade apple pie in one hand and a seven-layer taco dip in the other.

"You were my fourth choice, Liz," Margaret joked back.

"I made the apple pie yesterday, and I just whipped up the taco dip before I came over. You like?" Liz said while displaying her items with a wide, cheesy grin.

Margaret laughed. "They look tasty. OK, let me go check on the girls, and you two get settled in. I was thinking we could hang on the back porch," Margaret said as she made her way to Harper and Abby's bedroom.

Sarah and Liz went through the cupboards, grabbed some dishes, utensils, and glasses, and headed to the porch.

As they walked out, their mouths dropped open.

Margaret had the lights turned out with candles lit all around the screened-in porch. There were white twinkle lights strewn up high near the ceiling, and small speakers played soothing retro jazz. A cool breeze wafted through the screens, blowing just enough to make you want to put a long-sleeved shirt on.

Margaret walked in just as Sarah and Liz were setting up the food.

"Margaret! It looks amazing out here," Sarah said as she dipped a chip into the taco dip.

"I brought these throw blankets to wrap around our shoulders and get cozy with since I foresee us out here for a while," Margaret said, throwing them on a chair.

After settling in, Margaret vented about work, the girls, and Paul, and it felt like a heavy weight was lifted off her, finally. The three of them talked and talked and indulged in the delicious food spread and wine.

An hour in, Liz sprang up out of her chair and exclaimed she had something to admit to.

"I didn't want to say anything. I actually hadn't planned on even bringing this up. Ever. But Greg and I almost got a divorce. We had the papers ready to be signed and everything."

"What?!" Margaret and Liz were both shocked. They appeared the perfect, happy couple. The kind everyone envied.

"Why?" Margaret asked with a look of concern. Greg was like a brother to her. She loved her brother-in-law. He always helped their parents with whatever they needed. He was like the son they never had. He was excellent with all the kids, and he was just fun to be around.

"Well, I was unhappy. I wanted to move back to Cape May, and he wanted to stay where we were, you know, an hour and a half from Cape May, but closer to the city. I finally just accepted that but became increasingly resentful. I started to be angry with him all the time. I wanted to be near my family and close friends. I was sick of being that far from everyone. As this resentment stewed over weeks and months, I ended up running into an old ex-boyfriend from high school while out with friends at this open mic night."

"You didn't. Please tell me you didn't …." Margaret cut in.

"Let me finish!" Liz said, annoyed. "Nothing happened. We didn't even kiss, but we talked for hours and hours. Can you cheat on someone by talking for hours and connecting with another man? Is that cheating?"

"I really don't know," Sarah said.

"Well, that night made me realize how nice it was to really have a man listen to me again. To understand where I was coming from. To maybe even compromise instead of squashing my hopes and dreams with his needs. I never told Greg about that conversation, but I did ask for a divorce the following week."

"This is insane. I can't believe I didn't know about this. Does Mom know?" Margaret asked.

"No, I didn't want to tell anyone because I wasn't proud of my decision afterwards." Liz took a gulp of wine. "What happened next was astonishing. The divorce papers must have really scared Greg, because he found a way to get his company to let him work from home, and he agreed to buy this Cape May house. We had a night where we talked and talked, just like I had with my ex that night, and we got so much off our chests. Like, years and years' worth of things, because we had never taken the time to really sit down, talk, and listen."

Sarah and Margaret were on the edge of their seats taking

it all in, intently staring at Liz while resting their heads on their hands.

"In a crazy way, everything that went down during that time brought us to this new higher level in our marriage. It broke us down and made us into new people. People who valued their marriage and life more. People who valued conversations with each other more. People who actually listened when the other spoke."

Sarah, the notoriously single friend, had her mind blown over the whole thing. "This is crazy, Liz. I'm so glad that it all worked out in the end."

"You know I love both you and Greg. I'm so glad that you guys worked everything out. He has always been like the brother I never had," Margaret laid back in her chair and closed her eyes. "Can you guys tell me something? Am I going to have an epiphany with Paul like Liz had? Is our marriage going to be way more amazing after this insanely hurtful absence?"

"There's really no telling," Liz replied. "It's different people, different lives, and different scenarios. And really, deep down, it's about what you want and what he wants. I think you're still discovering what you want."

Margaret nodded, sat up, and took a long sip of wine.

"I haven't told you guys about this guy at work, Dave. There isn't much to say. We barely talk. I barely know him, but the other day I got those butterflies in my stomach when I saw him. I haven't experienced that in so long, and with everything going on right now, it felt amazing. It really got the wheels turning in my head. You know, about my marriage."

* * *

The next morning, Margaret groggily shuffled downstairs to make some coffee. She had a lot of things she wanted to get done early before getting the girls off to school and going to work.

She wanted to research the land her sister and Greg had just bought. It was all so fascinating. Liz wanted to do the research with her, but Margaret figured she'd get a head start. She opened her laptop, took a sip of hot coffee, and started an internet search. She loved this stuff. She was the Sherlock of the internet. She could whip up any information on a new guy her friend or family may have been dating with a quick search. She always spent time to find the best product with the best reviews for whatever it was she was looking for. She would spend hours researching restaurant reviews and looking at photos of the food to find the best places to eat. She was a little *too* into research at times.

After she typed in the address, some old photos popped up of the farm that had been on the land. There were pictures of little boys in overalls holding baskets and helping their granddaddies and fathers pick vegetables. There were photos of older women cooking and canning over hot stoves. Snapshots of tractors, farm animals, cats, and dogs. The farm had been called Piping Plover Farms. It had to have been twenty-five or thirty years since it was a working farm. Some photos revealed the beautiful wetlands across the street, which is probably what gave the farm its name. It looked like the owners prior to Liz and Greg didn't maintain much of the land except the area around the house. It explained why everything was so run down.

Margaret was super curious about the farm stand along the road and what it used to look like, but she couldn't find much on the internet. That would require more extensive research, including diving into some forums or local social media groups. She decided to wait to research more with Liz.

Closing her laptop, she took out a pen and notebook. She had to figure out finances while her hours were cut. Perhaps a side hustle? Her saving grace was she'd always been good with finances. There was enough money stored away that she could get by for another few months, and maybe by then she'd have her regular hours back. She had worked so hard her entire life, maybe she didn't need to stress about a little extra time off right now. Maybe she should relish it. Or maybe she could take this time off to really hone in on a new skill and a way to make extra income. There was a lot to think about. She'd start by writing a to-do list:

1. *Figure out other money-making avenues*
2. *Do more fun things with the girls*
3. *Spend more time in the garden*
4. *Spend more time at the beach and discovering new things*
5. *Research and brainstorm Liz and Greg's land*
6. *Figure everything out ...*

CHAPTER FOUR

"Here, girls!" Judy motioned to Margaret and Liz as they walked into their favorite local brunch spot that overlooked the ocean and beach. She occupied a table in the back, wearing a big floppy sunhat and huge sunglasses.

Judy was early to everything and always carried a book with her to read while she waited for others. Bob may have even dropped her off a little extra early so he could arrive to his favorite antiquing shops right when they opened.

Today was Margaret's day off, and the girls were at their friend's house having a sleepover. That meant it was a perfect day to hang out with her mom and sister.

"Sit, Sit! Let's order some delicious food and discuss our annual family reunion," Judy said.

Margaret and Liz gave each other mutual eye rolls and sat down. Their mother loved to plan. Sometimes even years in advance. It got to be overwhelming. While the sisters did plan things, they both enjoyed being more spontaneous, allowing for ideas and plans to come naturally or even at a moment's notice.

Everyone ordered and the dishes came out quickly.

Margaret got the bananas foster french toast special. Liz ordered an egg white omelet with asparagus and Swiss cheese, and Judy had her usual two eggs over easy with home fries, toast, and a fruit bowl side.

The ocean breeze was amazing. The sun was hot, but they were sitting in a screened-in porch that made for the perfect shade while not disrupting the view.

"So, what I'm thinking for our family get-together with my side of the family this year is this: instead of a week in the Poconos mountains, like we do every year, why don't we have everyone stay at your Great Aunt Mary's bed-and-breakfast here in Cape May?"

"Huh?" Margaret said with a furrowed brow.

"Since when does Aunt Mary own a B&B in Cape May? How have I never known this?" Liz said.

"She and Uncle Lou inherited it from his parents last year, and she was never fond of the beach or that B&B, so she didn't tell many people about it. In fact, she never really brought up the B&B when the in-laws owned it. She didn't get along well with them."

"Mom, this is not like you. The reunion is a little over a month away and the Poconos place is already booked. Do you really want to make everyone change their plans now?" Margaret asked.

"I've already spoken to everyone else, and they're all excited to do something new for the reunion. They won't have to change plane tickets since they'd fly into Philadelphia either way," Judy said.

Judy had five siblings, and all of them had spouses and kids of their own. Then, some of Margaret and Liz's cousins had kids that were around their kids' ages as well. It was about thirty people altogether. They lived all over the country and this was one of the few times of year they were all able to get together. They always had a blast too, gathering during Fourth of July week every year.

They typically rented an enormous house in the Poconos, and the kids usually slept on air mattresses in the living room. There were a few bedrooms and a huge loft with a ton of queen beds—it felt like one gigantic sleepover for the adults. The kids loved it. They got their sleeping bags lined up next to each other and they would make forts, watch movies, and tell ghost stories and play games. Days would be spent out on pontoon boats or hiking different trails. It really was a great place.

"So, who has been running this B&B if Aunt Mary wanted nothing to do with it?" Liz asked

Aunt Mary was Judy's mother's youngest sister. While Judy's mother, their grandmother, had passed away years ago, Aunt Mary was a young seventy-five. In fact, Aunt Mary was more like a big sister than an aunt to Judy since they were so close in age.

"Nobody's been running it. It's been vacant since they inherited it. They still have all the utilities on and have kept up with a little maintenance on it. They've just been letting friends and family stay there, and occasionally staying there themselves, but it's not currently a functioning bed-and-breakfast, that's for sure. I spoke with Aunt Mary a week ago, and she told me everything. She offered it to us for the reunion."

Margaret and Liz loved their Great Aunt Mary. She had never had kids, so she always had extra time to spend with them growing up. Even though she was technically their great aunt, it was easier just to call her aunt. She and Uncle Lou had a lot of money from running a successful business. That may have been part of the reason why this B&B wasn't something worth keeping to them.

"I mean, I'd rather go to the Poconos since I already live in Cape May and see it every day, but I think it will be fun to show our family around the place I love, especially the kids who haven't been here yet," Margaret said.

While they finished up brunch and paid the bill, Liz got an

idea. "Hey, why don't you show us Aunt Mary's B&B? I would love to see it. Is there anyone there now? Can we walk inside and take a look, or at least drive by?"

Judy lowered her sunglasses. "Well, I haven't actually seen it myself. Let me text her to see if it's OK if we swing by. I think there's a hidden key we can use. Give me a minute."

Margaret and Liz exchanged wide-eyed expressions of subdued excitement. Cape May was known for the most beautiful bed-and-breakfasts and Victorian houses. People came from all over to stay at the colorful B&Bs, frequent the shops, visit the beaches, eat at the restaurants, or go birding. Birders came to Cape May, which had some of the best bird watching anywhere, all year round. Autumn was especially magical as the migrating monarch butterflies, songbirds, and hawks all made pit stops in Cape May.

"OK, she sent me the address and told me there's a key we can use. Let's get on with it. I don't want to keep your father out antiquing too long or we'll have a ton more bagpipe records and rusty nautical items floating around the house. That man loves to shop more than me," Judy said, laughing.

It was true. Their father had a serious shopping problem, and when online shopping became big, it got messy. Literally. He was ordering anything that was on sale simply because it was a bargain, regardless of whether he or anyone else, actually needed the item. They had to have an intervention and weekly yard sales to remove the clutter. Luckily, he was much better these days about spending frivolously.

Piling into Margaret's car, they headed into town. It made sense that's where the B&B would be since a lot of them lined the streets there near all the shops.

Judy squinted at the street name when they pulled up to at the stop sign. "Oh wait, we have to turn around. It's not this way. It's over on Beach Avenue."

Margaret and Liz turned to look at each other, their

mouths open. Beach Avenue was where the enormous, super-expensive Victorian bed-and-breakfasts were. They faced the beach. Celebrities owned some of these houses. They were the ones you saw on all the postcards of Cape May, with the beach and ocean right out in front of them.

"OK, Mom, let me know when we're getting close," Margaret said as she rubbernecked each beautiful house they passed.

The Victorian houses were painted with beautiful colors. One house was purple, another pink, the next a light-green, and then yellow, and blue, and on and on.

"This is it. This is it." Judy pointed to a dark-blue house with pink-and-white striped awnings up ahead.

Margaret pulled into the driveway before they all got out and marveled at the house. A lot of the houses and B&Bs were named in Cape May, and this one had a sign out front that said The Seahorse Inn. On the sign, a painting of a horse wearing a wreath around its neck decorated with seahorses and flowers.

"Mom! This place is amazing. Like, a few million dollars amazing. Aunt Mary and Uncle Lou were just given this? This is insane," said Liz as she eyed the place up.

At the front of the house was a working fountain and bird bath where birds were taking their daily dips. There were thick pink and purple hydrangea bushes bordering the entire walkway and house. On the side of the house you could see bright-pink Knock Out roses, which popped nicely next to the blue of the house.

"Oh, let me grab the key. She said it would be around in the rear. I'll be right back," Judy said as she walked off.

Margaret and Liz trekked up the walkway to the stairs leading to the front porch. It was a big, beautiful wraparound affair, with rocking chairs and seating areas presumably for the guests who used to stay there.

Standing in front of the door, they turned around to take in the view. It was spectacular. They were high enough up to see past the dunes to the big blue ocean and sandy beaches.

"Wow. Just wow," Margaret said

"I know. I just can't believe it. This house has to be at least a few million. I thought only super rich people and celebrities owned these, but here Aunt Mary is among them," Liz said, placing her hands over her mouth in disbelief.

Margaret laughed. "Well, Aunt Mary and Uncle Lou are kind of rich, but that's beside the point."

When Judy returned with the key and they let themselves in, they discovered it was just as beautiful on the inside as it was on the outside. The house was so romantic, making it the perfect getaway for couples. Splitting up, they went in different directions to explore the house. There were nine bedrooms, each with a private bathroom.

"Mom and Margaret, can you come down here? I want to show you something," Liz called out excitedly.

As Margaret and Judy made their way downstairs, Liz pointed towards the kitchen.

While the rest of the house had an old-world charm, the huge kitchen had been remodeled and updated with stainless steel appliances and a large island with stools and a sink, many windows lined the walls, allowing sunshine to pour in.

"This kitchen will be perfect for our reunion. We won't be stepping all over each other like we do in the Poconos when we prepare dinner together," Liz laughed.

"And the dining room with the extra-long tables and lots of chairs will be great for our big family," said Judy.

"Oh my goodness. Come look at the living room. It's dreamy," Margaret yelled.

There was a working fireplace, built-in bookshelves, Victorian-style couches, an enormous chandelier, bronze candelabras on every shelf, and thick drapes on the windows that hung down to the floor.

"I feel like I just walked onto an old movie set. This is the neatest thing ever," Margaret said.

Liz had already walked back into the kitchen. "Did you guys even see what's out back yet?"

Margaret and Judy, still admiring the beauty of the living room, quickly walked into the kitchen to see what Liz was talking about. From the kitchen windows you could see a large deck and past that was a massive in-ground swimming pool with lounge chairs around the perimeter.

"Amazing. Let's get out there and look." Margaret rushed past them to get to the back door.

Once in the backyard, not only was there a deck and a pool, but a small greenhouse on the other side of the house, and what looked like a well-kept garden plot along the perimeter of the back fence at one time.

"Woah. I bet they grew a lot of their own food here for the meals they made the guests," Margaret said.

"OK, girls, this place is amazing. We'll surely be able to explore it all when we have the reunion in July, but we do need to hurry along. Your father is on his way to get me by now, and I told Mary I'd lock the place back up."

They secured the house, full of excitement in thinking of how blown away their extended family would be when they got there.

"Just maybe our cousins will fall in love with Cape May and want to move here," Liz said half-jokingly.

* * *

"Hey, do you want to come in and we can research my land online?" Liz asked as Margaret pulled down her long driveway. "Greg is out helping a friend with a project and the boys are at a long soccer practice."

"Oh, I forgot to tell you that I started to do some research on my own the other day. I found photos of the family who owned it. The farm stand was called Piping Plover Farms," Margaret said.

"That is so cool. I want in on this research, though. You can use the kids' laptop and I'll use mine. How about that?" Liz couldn't contain her excitement.

"I don't know. Today felt like a lot, and I really just want a long shower and to watch some mindless TV," Margaret said while lolling her head on the seat's headrest.

"Look, I have homemade apple pie and some freshly brewed iced tea. We can get comfy on the couch downstairs. Just stay an hour and then you can get home in time to relax and wind down."

"OK, fine," Margaret said, turning off the car.

Pie sliced, tea poured, they settled in with laptops, pens, and notebooks.

"So maybe if I search 'Piping Plover Farms' instead of the address this time, I'll find better information," Margaret said.

"And I'm going to type in the address with some specific keywords to see what I come up with," Liz replied.

"I think I found something. Look at this. It's a photo of the actual farm stand. I can tell it's the same one because of where it's located in the photo, right near the road and by that huge oak tree." Margaret pointed to a photo on her laptop.

"How cool. Read it to me."

"Piping Plover Farms had been in business eighty years. Passed down from generation to generation until the entire property was sold in 1995. The last family to run the farm decided to sell it instead of passing it down. The farm stand was open spring, summer, and fall, selling what they grew on the property. The stand also offered freshly baked goods, canned items, seedling plants, and potted and fresh-cut flowers. It was a favorite place to shop for many in Cape May.'

"Oh my gosh, how interesting is that? Look here," Margaret said.

She pointed to a photo of a large family in the '80s. There were the grandparents, mother, father, two daughters, and three sons.

"Is this the last family that ran the working farm, I wonder?" Liz asked.

"Seems so by the date of the photograph."

"Does it give any names? I wonder if we went to school with any of the kids."

"No, it just says 'Piping Plover Farms,'" Margaret said while staring at the screen.

"If this place was around while we were growing up, how come we don't remember it?"

"Well, I'm assuming it's because our parents never shopped at farm stands, only the grocery store. Also, we were young and probably didn't pay attention to these things back then. We were more interested in crimping our hair, teasing our bangs, and roller skating," Margaret said, laughing.

"That makes sense," Liz said before gasping. "Oh, now, here are some images of the chicken coops I found back in the forested area. Look how beautiful they were. The land was so neatly kept back then. Do you think they can be repaired, or will they need to be rebuilt?"

"I'm guessing that wood might be rotted, but who knows," Margaret replied. "Here's a photo of what the farm looked like. They grew a lot of corn."

"Who's that standing there, I wonder?" Liz asked.

Further back in the photo, a teenage-looking boy with long hair, ripped jeans, a frayed jean vest with patches adorning it, and black boots stood holding a basket of tomatoes.

"Oh my. He looks the opposite of what I pictured a farm boy to look like. But knowing us, he looks like one of those bad boys we were drawn to back then. I wonder if he had a loud motorcycle," chuckled Margaret.

"That is hysterical. I feel like we should know him from

school or something, but he doesn't look familiar at all. He probably was a bit older than us," Liz said.

"Yeah, you're probably right."

All of a sudden, both of their phones flashed a weather warning.

Weather alert: Thunderstorms likely for tomorrow.

CHAPTER FIVE

"So, you decided to show up, eh?" Dave said with a half-smile as Margaret walked towards the hospital. It felt like forever since she'd last seen Dave.

She smiled and nodded, not quite ready for a witty comeback, but feeling very grateful to see him, especially with everything going on.

"How's it been here for you, Dave? I feel like we haven't talked much."

Dave shook his head and looked into the distance at nothing. "Well, my hours got cut in half, so there's that. You?"

"Yep. Same. I really hope the donations pick up, not only for our jobs' sake but for the wildlife and community. They need our help," Margaret said.

Dave nodded, threw a ladder over his shoulder, and headed towards the deer enclosures by the lake before stopping abruptly and turning around. "Hey, have you heard anything about this storm we're getting tonight?"

Margaret, not expecting him to turn back toward her, quickly pretended like she'd been walking and hadn't stopped to stare at how strong his shoulders looked. "Yeah, I heard we're getting a thunderstorm, but that's all I know. We got alerts on our phones last night, and I've heard a little on the radio about it. Just seems like a typical thunderstorm. I guess it's a big deal because we've had such a dry spell lately," Margaret said.

"Quite possibly." Dave said, walking away.

Hopping into her car after a long shift, Margaret turned on the radio just as an alert was going off. *Severe storm warning in effect until midnight.*

Margaret hadn't heard anything about a severe storm happening tonight, just the normal ole thunderstorm. It was already nine o'clock, and if there was going to be a severe storm, she would have to make sure a lot of things were safely put away on her property. She must have missed all of this because of how busy they'd been at the hospital. Not to mention the cell phone reception was terrible because of how deep in the woods they were.

She called Dave to let him know what was going on so he could get the refuge's animal enclosures prepared for the storm.

"Hey," Dave said.

"Hi, Dave. Just curious if you've heard about the now *severe* storm warning in effect until midnight."

Dave let out a big sigh. "Yeah, I just heard. I've been rushing around battening down the hatches and making sure all the resident animals are safely tucked away in their enclosures. I had to go fix a few things at the deer pens."

Margaret breathed a sigh of relief. "OK. Please let me know if there's anything you need. In the meantime, I have to rush home and make sure all of my kids, animals, and plants are safe for the night.

"Will do. Stay safe."

Margaret called her mom, who was watching the girls for her. "Mom, we're in for a severe storm. I don't want you driving in it. Are the girls OK?"

"Oh I know, dear. I brought the girls to my house as I

didn't want to be on the road later. I called you and left a message, it kept going to voice mail. They are calling for up to sixty-mile-per-hour winds. It's not going to be pretty."

Judy was always on top of the weather. She watched the news daily and subscribed to a ton of different weather apps on her phone in order to keep a close eye on the radar and inform everyone when something was coming. She would have made for an amazing meteorologist.

Margaret rushed home to prepare for the storm at her own house. She needed to make sure her chickens were safely in the coops and locked up, and that all chairs and breakables were put away in the garage due to possible damage from the high winds.

It felt like a race against time at this point because the storm felt very close. The wind had picked up, and the air felt different. She had the windows partly down in her car and the radio up for any new information. A misty chill sent goose bumps prickling over her skin. Tiny little raindrops started tapping the windshield. She could tell something big was definitely about to happen.

Over the last few years, Cape May had started getting more and more tornado warnings during these storms, and it had gotten scary at times. She was worried about all of her delicate plants and vegetable seedlings being drowned out or ripped from the ground by high winds. There wasn't much she could do about that except make sure everything was tied up and staked well, but even that wouldn't guarantee anything.

On the other hand, Margaret loved rain and storms. She was fascinated by the work of Mother Nature and would often watch videos of tornados and hurricanes. She dreamed of being a tornado chaser, though there probably wouldn't be much to chase in her area. She enjoyed sitting on her screened-in porch during thunderstorms to listen to the rain and thunder while relaxing with a drink or book. Rain nourished the earth and her gardens, even though it was sometimes destructive. Rainstorms were one of the best things for her to fall asleep to as well. She loved rain and thunder storms, but not tonight. Not when she had just poured hours and hours of work into her garden and yard.

She arrived home and rushed to the backyard, passing Paul's car in the driveway.

No time to see why Paul's car was there, instead she worked feverishly to make sure all her chickens were locked in the coop and to get anything that was loose or valuable put safely away. She stacked all her outdoor chairs and put them in the garage. Then she grabbed her bird feeders, wind chimes, and ornamental glass balls and put those safely away as well.

The rain came down in sheets by the time she'd finished, and the wind had picked up considerably. It reminded her of a tornado or hurricane. The big oak trees in the neighbor's yard were practically bending in the wind, looking like they could snap in half. Margaret felt like a tree was about to fall on her and it now felt very dangerous to be outside. There was no time to check her seedlings or other plants. It was time to run inside and escape this scary storm.

She saw the lights flickering on and off in the windows as she ran back to the house. She had no idea where Paul was or why he suddenly decided to come back. As Margaret got to the back door, she was pelted by large balls of hail just as she stepped inside. Her stomach dropped knowing that her little seedlings were probably done for. Gardening gave her both great joy and disappointment every year. Right now, disappointment reigned.

Margaret kicked off her boots and snatched the paper towels she kept by the door to dry off just as a hand offered her a towel. She grabbed it in a hurry, drying off her face, neck, and arms. She was drenched from head to toe.

Meanwhile, Paul stood before her in a Hawaiian shirt, cut off khakis, and sandals. He normally wore button-down work shirts, slacks, and loafers. He looked like a stranger to

Margaret. There was a different aura to him. He wasn't the Paul she knew. This was a different Paul. He had let his hair grow longer for the first time in twenty years and had a mustache. He wore a different cologne. He looked different. *Everything* felt different. Margaret was at a loss for words. Was he just going to stand there, or was he going to say something? He'd left for a month with nothing but a note. After fifteen years of marriage.

The lights continued to flicker before snapping off altogether.

"Great. Help me light some candles, please, so we can see," Margaret murmured. Paul still hadn't said a word, but at least he hurried around the house, closing windows and lighting candles. Margaret loved candles, so they were everywhere. Luckily, she even had a lot of battery-operated ones that had popped on from their set timers.

Thunder boomed louder than she'd ever heard. Lightning flashed across the sky, and the gutters worked overtime to transport the overflow of water, a flash flood would not be surprising at this rate. The rain came in sideways, already soaking the ledges and floors by the windows by the time they could close them.

Then came tornado warnings as their phones called out with alerts. Sirens wailed at the local fire station in the distance.

Margaret motioned for Paul to follow her. "Let's get in the basement until this tornado warning passes."

Carrying some candles into the partially finished basement, she plopped in a chair, exhausted from running around. Paul stopped at the bottom of the stairs and sat on a step.

"Why are you suddenly here?" Margaret asked.

She kept her voice firm and confident as she didn't want Paul to think she was weak and had fallen into shambles after he'd left. After all, she hadn't, had she?

"I came to talk to you. I know I walked out. I know I shouldn't have just left a note. It was the only way I knew I could break away for time alone without being talked out of it. I needed this time for myself, for us, to truly see if this is working. I stayed at Will's family cabin in the Poconos. I turned off my phone and read books, fished every day, and took hikes. I did things I haven't done since I was a boy with my dad. I told my job that I needed a sabbatical, and they obliged. I needed to find myself again, find my inner child, and to find my dad within myself. I needed time to figure out what is happening between us, as well."

Paul's father had passed away a couple years before, and Paul had taken it incredibly hard. Margaret noticed a big change in him since it happened. She had recommended therapy to help him cope with the loss, but Paul was too hardheaded about it. It was all catching up to him in a big way.

Margaret suddenly felt sad for Paul, knowing how much he must have been going through to run away for a month. Then again, Margaret had her own issues in life and she never ran from them. She would never have left the girls or Paul for a month without even so much as a call.

Margaret took a long breath. "You hurt me when you left. I didn't know where you were or what was happening. I told myself that it was over, that we were done. I started the process of moving on. I know we don't have a perfect marriage. Far from it. But I really wish you had let me know what was going on. Not to mention what you put the girls through. All of this has affected them greatly. They haven't heard from their father in over a month. Abby's school performance went down—I got a call from her teacher."

"I am so sorry, Margaret" Paul said with a shaky voice. "I should have communicated. I should have been a better husband and dad. I was just … scared. I was afraid …"

Margaret looked down and shook her head. She didn't understand how he could leave his family for a month. Then again, he was immensely affected by his dad's death. It made sense. He never got over it. He never got the help he needed, and he only pushed those who tried to help him away.

An alert sounded on their phones again, this time notifying them that the tornado warning was over.

"Look, I don't want to discuss this now," Margaret said. "I have done a lot of thinking myself, though, and I have my own thoughts on the matter. You can sleep in the guest room tonight. There are clean sheets already on the bed. I just need my sleep right now, and I need to be alone."

* * *

She'd barely gotten any sleep that night. She'd laid awake for hours thinking of what she wanted and what was best for the girls and their family.

The next morning, as sunlight poured through the bedroom windows, Margaret sprang out of bed super early to go see what damage the storm had done. As she made her way to the garden, she saw that most of her new seedlings were drowned out and ripped apart from the rain, hail, and winds. A neighbor's tree had fallen onto part of her property and crushed her flower bed, and her vegetable garden looked totally wiped out. She felt defeated and discouraged. So much work down the drain. But such was life as a gardener. The plus side was that it was still May, and she had time to get a new set of crops in.

As she made her way back to the house, Paul was walking out to meet her.

Margaret motioned for him to sit on the bench next to her. "I have thought long and hard about this over the past month, and I think you need to find somewhere to stay until you can find a new place to live. This marriage has been on its last wheels for a few years now, and I think we've stretched it out long enough. I don't hate you, and I know you don't hate me, but I do know that we have grown to be two totally different people. We've grown apart, not together. I guess what I'm saying is … I want a divorce."

Paul looked at his feet. "I guess you're right. It's not what I want, but if it's what you want, I can't stop you. I think Will's family cabin is still available. I can probably stay there while I look for a place." He paused and turned to Margaret. "Are you sure about this? Is this really what you want?"

Margaret nodded.

There was sadness in his eyes, and Margaret felt it too. She could tell this was not what he wanted. However, she knew this had to be done. Their marriage was based on comfort, not passion or love, the last few years. Paul going away was just the straw that broke the camel's back, really.

"I want you to spend time with the girls. They need their father right now. My mom took them to her house last night, but they should be back by this afternoon. They will be so happy to see you. Maybe you can take them to the zoo and get ice cream afterwards or something," Margaret said trying to lighten the mood. "They need some one-on-one Dad time after this month."

* * *

Something changed in her after he left. After the sadness and shock had subsided, and survival mode kicked in, she'd started feeling like herself again. She felt a freedom and happiness that she hadn't experienced in a long time.

She didn't hate Paul. She still loved him. Deeply. But that love had changed. She no longer felt in love with him. In fact, she hadn't felt in love with him for years, but she kind of just pushed those thoughts aside so they could raise their girls in a two-parent household, the way she had been raised.

They had barely shown each other any affection in a long time, and she was starting to long for those wonderful hugs from behind. The kind where she'd be standing there, unsuspecting, when suddenly big strong arms would wrap around her. Paul had never really done that. Her high school boyfriend had though, and the feeling of it always stuck with her. To be an independent woman, but to also crave the comfort of a man's arms. It was that fluttering again. That sensation that elicits that butterflies-in-your-stomach reaction. That's what those hugs felt like.

Margaret suddenly felt a tinge of excitement at the thought of that happening again someday.

To feel in love again.

CHAPTER SIX

Click-click-click. Margaret turned her key in the ignition again. It was completely silent except for the clicks. Her car was not starting. Problem was, it was pitch-black at 9 p.m. and she was trying to leave work. The hospital had been locked up, and everyone else had gone home. She was stuck.

She couldn't get a cell signal either. She grabbed the flashlight that she kept in the glove compartment and started walking to where she might get better reception. No luck. Too deep in the woods. She decided to go back into the hospital and use the landline to call her mother.

"Mom, hi. I'm having car issues and my cell phone isn't getting service. I'm still at work. I can't get my car to start. I'm fine, though."

"Oh no!" her mom said. "Have you called a tow or car service?"

"Not yet, calling them after I hang up with you. Can you stay with the girls until I make it home? Not sure when that will be though."

"Most definitely."

Margaret searched her wallet for the membership card she

kept for the car service program she belonged to. Thankfully, she still had a month left on it before it expired.

She called but found out it would be upwards of three hours for them to get someone out to her. She texted her Mom to let her know.

Margaret walked back to her car to grab her sweatshirt when she felt a hand on her shoulder. She jumped, screaming louder than she ever had in her life.

"It's just me," Dave assured her evenly. "I saw from my window that you were still here and figured something may have been wrong, so I came to check." Dave held a bright flashlight pointed at the ground.

Dave lived in a house by the lake. It was owned by the wildlife refuge and he paid rent to live there. It had been rented by the prior person in Dave's position as well. It was a pretty good deal, as the rent was very cheap and you didn't have to go far to get to work.

"Oh my gosh, am I happy to see you. I just called the car service, and they said it will take three hours to get out here. Unbelievable"—Margaret shrugged—"but what can I do?"

"Look, I'd give you a ride home or try to jump your car, but my truck is also having issues at the moment. I haven't had a chance to get it towed to my mechanic yet. Living on site means I barely need to use it. Do you want to wait at my house? I can get some hot coffee or tea for you."

Margaret hesitated. Was she comfortable going inside his house? She had worked with him for many years, even though they rarely talked. But her alternative was waiting alone in the dark or going back in the hospital. She was quite curious of him and the house he rented at the refuge.

"Well, I was just going to wait inside the hospital or my car, but I think you sold me with a hot cup tea. They don't have that in the hospital."

"Great, follow me."

As Margaret followed him down the trail, a million crickets sang their song, accompanied by a chorus of frogs. There was a slight breeze, and little droplets of gentle rain began to fall, splattering on the leaves of the trees and sprinkling her arms. The air smelled like a mixture of pine, earth, and campfire. Margaret took a deep breath and blew it out, releasing all her tension and stress.

"OK, here we are," Dave said as he opened the door. "I was hoping we could hang on the deck overlooking the lake, but that doesn't look likely."

He removed his shoes just inside the door, and Margaret, not wanting to be rude, also took her shoes off.

After all these years, Margaret had never been inside this house. She'd expected something of a bachelor-looking pad or a run-down cabin, but this was something else.

"Oh, Dave. This place is incredible. You've really made yourself a nice home here. Did you do all of the work?"

"Yes, as a matter of a fact, I did. I offered to work on the house, and they were grateful since there wasn't really much in the budget for it. I enjoy fixing things up, so it was win-win," Dave said with pride. "They paid for most of the materials and I provided the labor. A lot of the materials I found from people who were giving them away, or for a super cheap deal. You know, like extras from a remodel project and so forth. I'll have to show you the before photos. It was pretty bad. The only part I haven't gotten to is the outside."

While the house had an older, somewhat shabby cabin look on the outside, the inside was completely remodeled. The kitchen had beautiful butcher block counters with white subway tile all the way up to the ceiling. A bay window sat behind the farmhouse sink. New black cabinets had been installed, as well as recessed lighting and deep-brown hardwood floors. And that was only the kitchen.

Margaret was amazed. Dave did have a job that entailed building things all day, so it made sense that the man knew how to build things. But still ....

"Here, take a seat in the living room, and I'll get some tea going," Dave said.

Margaret took in the mid-century modern living room adorned with the most cozy avocado-green couch, leather recliners, a few brass lamps, and massive pieces of artwork on the walls.

"Wow. Did you paint these?" Margaret asked, still completely impressed.

Dave looked over from cutting a lemon for the tea. "Yes, I did. A lot of them are of resident animals here on the refuge. I have some more that I never hung that are in the back room too. That one right there is my favorite," he said, pointing to a gorgeous three-by-three-foot painting of a barn owl.

"Dave, you need to showcase these. They are fantastic. You could easily sell these paintings. They are so unique and definitely make a bold statement," Margaret said, studying each painting.

"Thank you so much. I've always been a little shy about my artwork." Dave placed two cups of hot tea on the coffee table along with two pieces of strawberry pie.

Margaret had never had a man make her tea before. In fact, she never really had a man cook for her at all. Although there was that one, single time Paul boiled some pasta and dumped a jar of tomato sauce on top. Did that even count?

Paul did not cook. Ever. When he was left to his own devices and had to make the kids a meal, he would pop frozen pizzas in the oven or take them out to eat at the local hot dog place. That was the extent of it.

Margaret sat comfortably in a leather chair with her legs folded beneath her in a lotus position and grabbed her tea. After a few cooling blows, she took a sip.

"I muddled some honey and lemon in there. How does it taste?" Dave asked, studying her face.

"Exquisite. Thank you," Margaret said as she took a gulp and looked back with a grateful smile.

Dave smiled back. "Good, I'm glad. I'm sorry if I haven't been very talkative at work. I've been going through a little rough patch in my life the past year," he said, taking a sip of tea.

"Really? So, have I."

Dave perked up. "Really? Care to share?"

"If you're willing to share in return," Margaret half-smiled.

"Well, I might as well get it out in the open to someone." Dave inhaled slightly before launching in. "Even though I've worked here for years, the reason I came to live here last year was because I was going through a divorce and it seemed like the best place for me to move to. It was available and they were more than happy to have me rent and redo the place … OK, your turn." Dave said abruptly.

Margaret took another sip. Her stomach knotted in anticipation of saying the words out loud for the first time. "I just asked my husband of fifteen years for a divorce. And when I say 'just' I mean that you are the first one to hear this. I haven't told anyone yet. It's been a roller-coaster month, to say the least. I'm curious about your divorce. Do you care to elaborate?"

Dave shifted in his seat and set his cup down. "Well, we were married for ten years. Never had kids. One day I got home from work early and decided to drive down to Tuckerton Lake to go fishing. As I was driving, I figured I'd stop and see if my friend Will wanted to join since I knew he had Tuesdays off. When I pulled up, my wife's car was in the driveway. I never said anything, just drove home because I was so upset. I decided not to jump to conclusions though. What if she was there planning a surprise party for me? Or dropping something off? When she got home, I asked how work was, but she didn't mention being at Will's house. At that point I just let it go. I decided to think optimistically about the situation. This was my wife and best friend, and I didn't want to think the worst. They would never do something like that, right? Well, a month later

I got home from work early again, about four hours early. This time, I pulled up to my driveway, and Will's car was in it. When I went into the house, they were nowhere to be found. In the kitchen, I could see out the window into the backyard. They were sitting out beneath the tree that we'd said our marriage vows under, holding hands and kissing. I couldn't believe it. So, that day I lost my wife and my best friend. I immediately asked for a divorce and cut Will out of my life. That night, I asked about moving into this place, and the next day, I was out of the home I shared with my wife. I couldn't bear to be there one more day."

Margaret put her hands over her mouth. "Oh my, I'm so, so sorry. That is horrible. Nobody should ever have to go through that."

Dave nodded and took a big bite of pie. "So, let's hear your story."

"Well, it's a lot more boring than yours. There wasn't any cheating involved. My husband wrote a note and just up and left. Didn't hear from him for a month. I was upset and angry, especially for our two girls, who were wondering why he left and hadn't called. I started reflecting about what marriage brought me and decided I wanted a fresh start. When he came home during the storm, I asked for a divorce. It was an awful day—my garden was also completely destroyed, but that's another story. I've already filed, and he's staying at his friend's place until he gets sorted out. We still have to have the talk with our girls."

"Oh. Man. Life is crazy, isn't it?"

Margaret's phone dinged with an incoming text, and she noticed the rain had picked up and it was pouring outside.

Due to weather conditions, you may experience delays with a service repair technician or tow truck driver.

"Now it looks like I might be waiting even longer than three hours, according to this text message. I thought midnight was pretty late as it was," Margaret said, yawning.

"Look, I can make you a nice setup on this couch. You can sleep, relax, or just wait until someone gets here. How about that? And if you want to just hang and talk, I'm game. I usually stay up pretty late anyway. I'm a horrible sleeper. I'll even go outside with you when he gets here so you're not all alone with a strange man in the woods."

"Oh, the irony," joked Margaret as they both laughed.

Dave was really starting to grow on her. He was a true gentleman who liked to take care of people it seemed. Not only that, he was very skilled, creative, and kind.

"So, tell me about this garden that got destroyed. I used to be super into gardening. Out here, with all these thick trees and not a lick of sunlight, gardening doesn't stand a chance. I miss it."

"Yes, it's my favorite hobby. I do a vegetable and flower garden every year. I spent so much time growing the seeds under lights and planting everything outside, then the storm wiped everything out. I have to start over, but I'm not sure what I'm going to do yet."

"Well, it's still early enough to get all your seedlings in again. Can you just buy the plants and seeds you need at the local nursery and replant them in your garden?"

"That's the thing. I could do that, but I have another option. My sister and brother-in-law just bought a house down the road from me in Cape May. It has acres and acres of land, and they have no interest in using all of it and have offered some to me. It would mean I could potentially grow more than I've ever dreamed of."

"That's exciting. What do you think you're going to do?" Dave asked.

"I think I'm going to start over on their property and plant the biggest and best garden ever. The funny thing is, the property is like a treasure hunt. There's an old abandoned farm stand and chicken coops that we are thinking about redoing and probably so much more back in the forest along the property. It was once a working farm."

Dave's eyes widened. "Wait a minute. Did you say this was in Cape May?"

"Yep. Over by me, close to Sunset Beach."

"Come here, I have to show you something." Dave motioned to the back room that he used as an office.

Margaret followed, spotting about five paintings stacked against the wall. "Oh, Dave. These are incredible."

Dave smiled. "They're of my family's farm."

Margaret looked at all of them and stopped dead in her tracks when she got to the painting of the house. "Gosh, this sure looks like my sister's new house."

"I think that's because it is."

Margaret's eyes widened. "Are you telling me that you grew up in my sister's house?"

"I'm starting to think so. Here's my painting of our farm stand. We loved working there as kids. We would play the radio, stock fruit and vegetables, tell jokes, dance, and meet the coolest people who stopped to shop on their way to vacation."

Margaret was blown away. "This is what that run-down farm stand used to look like? It's beautiful. How did it ever become what it is now?"

"My parents retired early from the farming business, and none of us kids wanted to keep it going. My one brother wanted to be a dentist, another brother got an office job, I wanted to be an artist, and my sisters all had their separate goals and dreams. There wasn't anyone to hand it down to. Sometimes I regret not taking it. They sold it off, but the people who bought it didn't keep up the farming business. They just let the land sit there and do nothing, and all of the structures just wasted away. It still makes me sad to this day."

"I can't believe this. I think they were the owners who sold it to Liz and Greg. Wait until my sister finds out. You know, we googled this farm to find out the history. Were you the boy I saw in the old photos, decked out with '80s big hair, torn jeans, and combat boots?"

Dave laughed. "Oh yes, that was definitely me. My parents wanted me to act and look like a farmer. That wasn't happening. I was an artist who expressed himself however he pleased. It made for lots of fun family arguments. I will say this, if you're thinking of bringing that farm and farm stand back to life, I'd be more than willing to take part in it with you. I would love nothing more than to work on my family's old property again. It would make me so nostalgic and happy, and it would finally get me off the refuge. I spend way too much time here, as you can tell. Not to mention the extra free time you and I are about to have with our hours being cut."

Margaret squealed and gave him a big hug. "You don't even know how happy you just made me. I've always had a dream of having a huge garden, and now it feels like it just might happen. I love my gardens at my home, but my yard has very limited areas of direct sunlight with all the trees. I've never been able to grow as much as I've wanted to for all these years because of it."

CHAPTER SEVEN

After a week, Paul and Margaret decided it was time to finally tell the girls about the divorce.

"Girls, your father and I have something to discuss. Please come sit in the living room," Margaret instructed.

Paul was already sitting in a chair, fiddling with his guitar.

"You know we both love you, right?" Margaret asked.

"Yes!" they cried in unison.

"You also know that Dad has been staying elsewhere for a bit, right?"

The girls both looked at each other and nodded.

"Well, Dad is probably going to continue living elsewhere, because while we still love each other, we just aren't happy living together anymore."

Paul was not really paying attention, still fiddling with his guitar. Margaret was getting annoyed with his lack of engagement during this super-important conversation that their daughters would probably remember their entire lives.

"Paul!" Margaret blurted out.

"Oh, um, yes. Yes. What your mother is saying is true. Do you two have any friends at school that have a mom and dad who live apart?" he asked.

"You mean a divorce?" Harper asked.

"Yes, dear," Margaret confirmed.

Abby started crying and Harper slapped her hand on her forehead.

"Does this mean we get extra presents at Christmas?" Harper asked.

Paul and Margaret glanced at each other.

"Well, there will probably be two Christmases for you to attend instead of one, and sometimes you might spend one holiday with Dad and one with me."

Margaret sat down next to Abby and let her crawl into her lap. She put her arm around Harper.

"We know this is going to be hard for you guys, but just know that you will both be taken care of and will still have all the love in the world from your parents, even though we will no longer be married and living together. You two and I will still live here in the house. Your father will be finding a new place to live."

"After school tomorrow we'll spend some time together," Paul reassured the girls.

* * *

Paul showed up the next day after school like he'd said, except he had a woman with him. A hippie-looking curly haired blonde with a flowy peasant top, long patchwork maxi skirt, multiple scarves around her neck, and strappy sandals. She smelled like a mixture of paint and patchouli. Had Paul already found someone?

"Margaret, this is Sandy," Paul said.

"Hi, Sandy. And who, exactly, may I ask, are you?"

Paul interrupted before Sandy could say anything. "A friend."

This was supposed to be special daddy-daughter time and he's already bringing a new woman around? A day after breaking the divorce news? This man's brain was absurd.

Margaret didn't like it, but what could she do? They were getting divorced. She could say something. Maybe she would. Maybe she wouldn't.

After the girls left with their dad and Sandy, Margaret *knew*. And although she knew, she still sought confirmation. Paul had left an old cell phone in the closet, and she knew it worked with Wi-Fi. He would let the girls use it sometimes to scour the internet from the couch.

She ran upstairs to find it. It was right where it always was in the basket on the top shelf of the office closet. She powered it on, connected to the Wi-Fi, and went to his mailbox, and thus, to all of his e-mails. Scrolling as fast as she could, she finally got past the junk to one from someone named Sandy. She scrolled even further to see how far the e-mails went, and she stopped at one from Sandy that caught her eye dated April 8 of this year, which was right before he left for a month.

Margaret opened the e-mail and started reading:

Hey, you! So, this is the link to the house Will and Michelle invited us to. A bunch of my other friends will be there. If you look at the photos, you can see how big it is. We'll have our own suite upstairs with a private bathroom. It's deep in the mountains, so cell reception might not be great. I can't wait. It's going to be so much fun to have you meet all of my friends and for us to finally not hide our love from others anymore.

Love,

Sandy

Margaret couldn't believe it. How long had this affair been going on? She kept scrolling until she found the first e-mail in December.

"December!" Margaret yelled out loud to nobody. "He's been having an affair since at least December! I can't believe it! I am so glad we are getting a divorce!"

Margaret read that first e-mail:

Hi, Paul. It was nice meeting you the other night at your friend Will's house. It felt like I could have talked to you for hours. Michelle said it was as though we were in our own little world in the corner since we weren't socializing with anyone else. You mentioned you might be able to help me put new strings on my guitar when you gave me your e-mail. I think I'm going to hold you to that. Maybe we can get together sometime for coffee.

Love,

Sandy

Well, there it was. The start of the affair. They met through Will, apparently. Did this woman not know that he had a wife and children? Who was Michelle?

Margaret knew Will was a work friend of Paul's but had only met him once when she picked Paul up from work one day. She knew virtually nothing about him.

The girls would be back in a few hours and Margaret was fuming. She didn't know what to do. Confront him? Confront him while he was with Sandy after the girls had gone inside? He had lied about everything. He hadn't gone away to have alone time to connect with his deceased dad. He was having an affair. And why had he seemed so sad when she asked for a divorce? Had he rethought the affair and wanted to rekindle the marriage that night of the storm?

After simmering down, Margaret called Sarah.

"What do I do, Sarah? Paul brought a woman with him to pick up the girls today. I did some snooping, and I found out he went to be with her for that month in the mountains. He lied about everything. He's been seeing this woman since December!"

"What? Yikes. I never saw that coming. However, you wanted a divorce before you knew any of this. Most people would want a divorce *because* of this. You wanted a divorce because you weren't happy or fulfilled in the marriage anymore. While what he did isn't right by any means, I think you just need to move forward with the divorce and go live your life. He doesn't need any more of your time, and at least you know the truth now."

"Maybe you're right, but I am itching to say something. I want him to know I know."

Sarah sighed. "It's not worth it. What good will it do? For you? For the girls? Will it have any positive effect? No. It will only get your adrenaline pumping and put your stress levels higher. It will cause conflict between Paul and yourself, and that will put stress on the girls. They don't need any more of that right now."

"Ugh. Why do you always have the best advice?" Margaret asked.

"Maybe that master's in counseling helped a little," joked Sarah.

As much as it pained her, Margaret decided to let it go, at least for now. She definitely didn't have any doubts about the divorce now though.

Paul, Sandy, and the girls arrived back around 9 p.m. They had gone out to dinner and stopped at the park to feed the ducks.

Margaret waved goodbye to them with a flick of the hand and brought the girls inside.

It was a perfect beach day. Since Margaret's hours were reduced to three twelve-hour shifts a week, and the kids only had a half day at school, Margaret and Liz decided to take the kids to Cape May Point.

Margaret and Liz grew up going to this beach. It was an ideal place to swim, as the waves were calm, making it feel more like a bay. Dolphins always swam by, and if you stayed late enough on the beach, which they loved to do, you could catch the most amazing sunset. A wide rock jetty beach extended out into the ocean, and many people would set up their umbrellas and chairs on it. That's where Liz and Margaret set up camp every time. It was right near the lifeguards, so it was the perfect spot to keep an eye on the kids.

They walked onto the sand and dropped everything in their spot. It was late May now, hot enough for the beach but without the crowds just yet. Droves of visitors would be coming in soon for Memorial Day weekend. Abby and Harper flung off their flip-flops and made a mad rush to the water near the lifeguard stand. Liz's boys chased after them with goggles hanging off their faces and boogie boards in their arms.

Margaret and Liz plopped their chairs in the sand and set up the umbrellas. Margaret had to have some shade and Liz liked to bake in the sun all day.

"Do you want a drink?" Liz asked, reaching into the cooler.

"Yeah, throw me a lime seltzer, please. Oh, boy do I have a lot to talk about today," Margaret said.

"Really? Do tell!"

"Well for starters, I found out Paul has been seeing someone else for a while now, at least since December. When he left for a month, he went to be with her and her friends in the mountains. I found out by snooping through his old phone in the upstairs closet."

"What?!" Liz sat straight up and tilted her sunglasses down. "Are you kidding me?"

"Nope. So, this divorce is happening, alright. Sarah advised me to just move on and not bring it up since we're already going through a divorce. She feels it might make things more stressful for the girls. I've already filed for a no-fault, so it is what it is. This way, we can be amicable and successfully co-parent them without any nasty legal battles. I'd rather have it this way."

"Ugh. I knew it. As soon as Mom told me, I knew something shady was going on. A man doesn't just leave for a month like that. You don't need a month to find yourself and connect with nature. That's insane. Greg and I both knew it, but we didn't want to upset you by bringing it up … and also because I wasn't supposed to know."

Margaret looked over at the kids in the water and scoffed. "Can you believe he acted sad when I asked for a divorce? He seemed like he wanted to make the marriage work that night. I guess he had second thoughts."

"Maybe he did. His loss."

"I do have something happier to discuss too," Margaret said with a smile. "I found out a ton of information about your farm from my coworker Dave. My car broke down and I had tea at his place on the refuge while waiting for the service technician to arrive. His family used to own the farm—he grew up there! They sold it to the people that sold it to you guys. He was very excited about helping me put a garden in and restore some things."

"You're kidding." Liz sat straight up again. "This is fantastic news. Can you bring him over sometime? We would love to meet him and hear about what our property used to be. You know Greg, he's super into history, and he'll definitely want to know everything. I can make dinner. We can let the kids play while the adults hang. How about it?"

"I think I might be able to persuade him. He's been going through a divorce too. We kind of bonded the other night. He can build the most amazing things, and his paintings are insane. You have to see them. He has paintings of the farm from when he lived there."

"How about tomorrow night?"

"That's kind of soon, no?"

"No, not really. You've known the guy for years. Just bring him over." Liz laid back down in her chair and stretched her toes in the sand.

Margaret liked the idea, but then thought about how she was mad that Paul was bringing another woman around the girls already. Though, Dave really was just a friend and coworker, unlike Sandy.

Later that night, Dave agreed to dinner at Liz and Greg's the next day.

"Oh, this is exciting," Dave said on the phone to Margaret. "My truck got fixed so I can meet you over there. Five thirty, you said?"

"Yep, and feel free to bring any things that might pertain to the house or land. They are very interested in learning all about what it once was."

"You bet. How about I bring over some of my homemade pie too?" Dave asked.

Margaret laughed. "That pie was amazing. You can definitely bring it."

* * *

Five thirty rolled around the next day, and Margaret and the girls had just pulled up to the house. The girls immediately jumped out of the car to play with the boys, who were already in the backyard.

Dave pulled in right behind her. He stepped out and looked around, seemingly taking it all in.

"Does being here again bring back a lot of memories?" Margaret asked.

"Oh yes. This is pretty surreal right now. I've missed being here," Dave said taking a deep breath in.

Liz and Greg both stepped out the front door with their dogs running past them to greet Dave and Margaret.

"Hi, Dave. I'm Liz, and this is Greg. So nice to meet you. How awesome that we're living in your family's old home."

Dave greeted them and shook their hands before handing them the pie. "Thank you so much for inviting me. Here's a strawberry pie I made."

Liz took the pie and discretely glanced at Margaret, silently mouthing, "*He's a good one.*"

Margaret had brought her famous caprese salad and

deviled eggs, and Liz whipped up the most scrumptious pulled-pork sandwiches, potato salad, pickled squash, and baked beans.

During dinner, Dave told some great stories about the farm and had even brought over some old newspaper articles and photos. Several of his stories had everyone rolling in laughter. Who knew farm kids had such a crazy fun life?

After dessert, Liz wanted to show him around.

"Would you like to walk around the property?" she asked.

Dave's eyes filled with excitement. "Oh, most definitely."

Starting in the backyard, they eventually made their way through the fields towards the trees.

"This is where we grew everything. We usually put the corn over there, squash here, strawberries over there, tomatoes just to the left there," Dave said, pointing in all directions.

Liz and Greg took it all in, holding hands as they followed Dave, absorbing all his descriptions. Margaret loved seeing them so happy.

"Ah yes, the chicken coops. We used to play hide-and-seek out here. I always hid in the chicken coops," Dave joked when they came upon them. The sun was completely set at this point and the sky was a dark pink, casting bruising purple shadows around the tattered structures.

They were nearly through the fields, headed back towards the house when headlights came up the driveway.

"Who's that?" Greg asked.

"Oh … I forgot. Paul asked to get the girls tonight for an hour. He's taking them for ice cream."

As they got closer, Margaret could see Sandy in the passenger seat again.

"Who's that in the car? With the blonde hair?" Liz asked.

Margaret kicked Liz and looked at her with widened eyes.

Liz immediately realized it was the woman Paul had cheated on her with.

"That's Sandy. She's Dad's friend," Harper informed her aunt as they approached the driveway.

Dave stopped. "You guys go on without me. I'll wait here."

Margaret looked back at him as he stared at the car.

After the girls hopped in and drove off, Margaret walked back over to Dave. "Is everything all right?"

"Well, remember I told you about my ex-wife? That woman, Sandy, in your ex's car … is her best friend," Dave said.

"Wait. What?" Margaret said, eyes as wide as saucers. "Hold on. This is starting to add up. I can't believe it."

Dave looked puzzled. "What are you talking about?"

"I haven't told you, but I found out Paul did in fact cheat on me. It was with that woman, Sandy. He doesn't know I know. He told me when he went away for a month that he stayed at his friend Will's house in the mountains to find himself. Turns out, he went away with her. I only met Will once, so I didn't know him well. I'm wondering if his friend Will from work is the same Will that was your best friend."

Dave pondered the idea for moment. "My ex's name is Michelle. Does that ring any bells?"

"Yes," Margaret intoned, "she talked about her friend Michelle in an e-mail. She said that Will and Michelle invited her and Paul to stay at the house in the mountains with them."

"So, they were all in the mountains together. Your ex and my ex. I was cheated on, and now you. You have got to be kidding me. This is unreal."

"Yes, it is. I feel like I'm in a movie. How about we go for a walk and then I pour us some hot tea."

"That sounds amazing right about now." Dave looked out towards the farm, then looked back at Margaret with a smile.

CHAPTER EIGHT

"We're whisking you away," Liz said, making room in her car's trunk.

Liz and Sarah arrived in Liz's car on a Friday morning with nothing but an hour's notice via text message.

Margaret had a look of uncertainty on her face. "I have a million things to do. I don't know if this is a good idea …."

"We don't know what your plans are, but you're coming with us. Let's help you pack," Sarah said as she walked towards the house.

"Greg is going to take the girls," Liz said as Greg pulled up with the boys in tow. "They can stay and play with the boys over the weekend. Greg's parents are here and want to take the kids fishing and to the carnival. I think it will be fun for them. If Paul is picking them up for something, then the guys can coordinate."

"Nope. Paul doesn't have them this weekend. All good there. The girls will be so excited about this," Margaret said cheerfully.

Liz knew Margaret had a three-day weekend because of her reduced work hours and had taken it upon herself to plan a girls' getaway.

"So, where are we going?" Margaret asked as she sipped her coffee.

"We'll tell you in the car. It's a surprise. Now go inside and get your stuff together, or Sarah's going to pack all of the wrong things for you. I think she's in there helping the girls get ready," Liz said laughing.

Abby and Harper came running out full speed with overstuffed suitcases and smiles on their faces. "We're so excited, Mom! Sarah just helped us pack," Harper squealed.

Greg hopped out of the truck and put Abby's and Harper's suitcases in the back. The boys ran out to greet the girls, and that turned into an impromptu game of tag all over the yard.

"OK, I'm headed out with the kids if everything is good here, but let me check your oil and tires first."

Liz blushed and smiled. "Thanks, Greg."

Greg always worried about Liz and her car on long drives. He would take it upon himself to make sure the oil level was good, and the tires had enough air.

Sarah walked outside with Margaret's suitcase filled to the brim.

"I told you to get in there and pack. Now you've got to wear whatever Sarah put in there," laughed Liz.

"What? I think I packed some good stuff, if you ask me," Sarah said.

Margaret chuckled as she made her way inside. "OK, well at least let me get my toiletries and some other things."

* * *

Margaret, Liz, and Sarah were finally on the road, headed to their destination.

"Since I can barely keep it in any longer, I'll tell you where we're going. We are doing a weekend in New York City. I booked reservations at a five-star hotel near Central Park, Sarah scored us tickets to a play, and I made some fabulous dinner reservations. I have plenty of other ideas of things for us to do, as well," Liz said excitedly.

They all clasped their hands together and squealed in unison.

"This is all too exciting, guys. I can't thank you enough for doing this," Margaret said.

"It's roughly a three-hour drive, so settle in, gals!" Liz said as she put the pedal to the metal.

They eventually pulled up to their hotel near Central Park. After leaving the car with the valet and baggage with bellman, they walked inside the superbly plush lobby, taking in the beauty of the huge crystal chandeliers that hung above polished marble floors from the vaulted ceiling. A gorgeous fountain sat in the middle of the space with plants all around it, and a glass beverage dispenser full of cucumber-mint water sat off to the side with cups at the ready.

Liz checked in before they proceeded to take the elevator up to the twenty-fifth floor.

Upon entering the room, the first thing they all noticed was the breathtaking view out of the floor-to-ceiling windows. You could see for miles across Central Park on the left, and the city buildings on the right.

"These views are insane and much better in person," Liz said.

"Ooh! These beds are so comfortable," Margaret practically moaned, sitting on one.

It was a two-bedroom suite with a kitchen and little living room. Everything was sparkling clean and elegantly detailed in the room, making it fit for a queen. The bedding was crisp white and fluffy, and the bathroom had a walk-in tiled steam shower. It felt so luxurious.

"I'm taking the pullout bed in the living room, you two have the bedrooms," Sarah said.

"Why don't you just share the king bed with me? I don't mind at all. It's plenty big enough," Liz countered.

Sarah laughed. "I'm fine out here. It's not a big deal at all. I'm happy to just be here!"

"OK, how about we freshen up and go grab some appetizers somewhere. It's only three thirty, so I don't want to spoil our appetites before our dinner reservation, but I'm starving," Liz said as she unzipped her suitcase and pulled out a sleeveless black sheath dress.

Margaret put on a long flowy blue dress and heels, something she hadn't worn in years. She hadn't dressed up like this since her cousin's wedding. "Thanks for packing this, Sarah. I've wanted to wear it again, but never had a reason to."

"I was hoping you would like that I put it in there," Sarah said, donning a bright-orange gauzy off-the-shoulder dress with sandals.

The cold air conditioning inside the hotel made them forget how sweaty they were going to get as they made their way outside in the city's summer heat.

"I was thinking we could take a cab somewhere for appetizers and drinks, and maybe we can change shoes and walk around Central Park before cabbing it to dinner afterwards?" Liz, ever the obsessive planner, had attended college in the city and took her first job as an interior designer in the Flatiron District. She knew all of the amazing little places to go and eat. Luckily, Margaret and Sarah were easygoing and happy to go with the flow.

A valet attendant offered to hail a cab for them, but Liz had already walked authoritatively to the curb and put two fingers in her mouth, eliciting a piercing whistle, while waving an arm. A cab came roaring up. Margaret and Sarah laughed hysterically.

"Hey, I'm a boy-mom. This whistle has come in handy wrangling my sons," Liz said matter-of-factly.

Liz told the cab driver where they were going, and within ten minutes they arrived at a little wine cafe that served tapas.

Outside, a man with a guitar played '70s soft rock, and almost every table was full under the sidewalk awning.

Liz walked ahead to put her name in with the host, and luckily, they had a table inside available. 1980s yacht rock played on the inside speakers, and all of the servers wore crisp-white shirts with black ties. There were beautiful paintings on the wall by different local artists with little price cards on each in case someone wanted to buy them.

"This is one of my favorite spots in the city for appetizers. They have tapas, which are those small dishes popular in Spain. I think you'll love it," Liz stated.

Margaret didn't suppress her mirth when she told her sister, "We know what tapas are," while Sarah cackled beside her.

"OK, just checking." Liz's shoulders shot to her ears and she put her hands up in a *I surrender* gesture.

Margaret and Liz were both big travelers and knew a lot about different foods. Margaret loved to visit new places not as a tourist but as a local. She tried to find all the hidden non-touristy treasures that only the community knew about. She would sit in cafes and strike up conversations with residents and find information on the most amazing restaurants.

They ordered some wine and food, and relaxed, enjoying the atmosphere and conversation. Margaret was feeling extra inspired lately, and this weekend trip was really the icing on the cake.

They cabbed it back to the hotel, changed shoes and clothing, and walked over to Central Park. The birds were chirping and so many people were spread out on the lush green grass reading, playing with their kids, or enjoying conversation with friends and family. This city had an energy to it that radiated through your soul. It felt like Margaret could be anybody she wanted to be here in NYC. It felt like the birthplace of inspiration and motivation. It was such a different kind of beauty, all this nature in this huge park right in the middle of the bustling city.

After spending an hour in the park, Margaret suggested they walk back to the hotel for showers and a little relaxing before they headed off to their dinner reservation. Liz still hadn't told them anything about where they were going for dinner.

By 8 p.m. they were all dressed up again and ready to cab it to dinner. This time, Liz let the valet attendant hail one for them. Liz told the cab driver where to go and they were off.

The cab pulled up to a grimy, seedy-looking building with one small window that had security bars on it and a bouncer sitting on a stool outside the door.

"This is it. Thank you," Liz said to the driver as she opened the door.

Margaret and Sarah hesitated, and didn't move from the cab.

"Liz, are you sure this is it? It sure doesn't look like *it*," Margaret said.

"Yeah, I'm feeling a wee bit overdressed for this place," Sarah seconded.

Liz laughed. "Oh, I'm sure. I've been here many times. Trust me. We're all dressed just fine. Wait until we get inside."

Margaret and Sarah looked at each other skeptically and reluctantly stepped out of the cab.

The bouncer checked their IDs, which made them all a little giddy, and they walked through the small front door into a dark room.

"Liz, I know we can find some better places to eat dinner than this," Sarah said as she eyed up the dark empty room without a soul in sight, just tables and a long wraparound bar.

"This isn't where we're eating. It's in there," Liz said, pointing to the back. There was a doorway with a thick velvet curtain draped across it. A man pulled open the curtain for them, stamped their hands, and told them the cover charge was ten dollars a head.

"I got this, guys," Liz said, getting out her wallet.

They crossed the threshold and stepped into a lively scene. A beautiful candlelit jazz club, full of couples and friends wining and dining, sprawled before them. They'd arrived during the set break, but there was a stage set up with thick red drapes behind it, soft spotlights, and instruments just waiting to be played. The walls were covered with framed photos of famous jazz musicians. Vintage-style Edison bulbs hung from the ceiling in mason jars, and the front of the stage had blue and purple uplighting on the drapes. A small dance floor was situated in front of the stage as well.

The three of them took their seats at a high-top table to the side. It was lit by a small votive candle, and they had to read their menus by the flashlights of their phones. They didn't mind, as the ambiance was wonderful. They each ordered a drink, an entree, and one appetizer to share. The menu looked exquisite, full of interesting and fresh items not seen normally, like stuffed squash blossoms, chilled pea soup with homemade croutons, and fig-and-brie flatbread with toasted pistachios and orange zest.

Eventually, someone got on the microphone onstage and introduced the band for their second set. Other jazz bands were in the lineup, too, spread out all the way into the wee hours of the morning.

A bunch of musicians filled the stage, and the next thing they knew, the whole place was bobbing, swaying, or dancing to the music. Couples got up out of their seats, taking to the dance floor, and even the bouncer by the curtain was bobbing his head to the music. Others stayed in their seats, just enjoying the sounds while they ate or drank.

"See, you two. I told you to trust me. I wanted to surprise you, so I didn't give out too many details. This is an old jazz club that I was introduced to in college, and it's still around doing its thing. Not many people know about it. Mostly locals. They are known for having some of the best jazz acts in the country," Liz said smiling.

"This is absolutely amazing. I've only seen these types of places in the movies, and the food is fantastic," Sarah said digging into a beautiful charcuterie board full of meats and cheeses, freshly made crackers, pickled vegetables, fresh fruit, and sides of truffle honey, tomato jam, and fig preserves.

Margaret held up her glass. "To us. To sisters and lifelong friends. To wonderful things in our future."

Liz and Sarah scrambled to lift their glasses too. "And to a beautiful, fresh start for you, Margaret!" Liz toasted.

Just before the kitchen closed at 1a.m., they ordered desserts: a piece of deconstructed lemon meringue pie with fresh mint, a piece of homemade key lime pie, and a piece of homemade chocolate cake with buttercream icing and fresh raspberries.

It was an evening to remember. By 2 a.m., they were ready to call it a night. They hailed a cab and headed to their hotel. They couldn't wait to get out of their shoes and dresses and into their pajamas.

Margaret checked her phone as she tiredly slipped in bed. She had a missed text message. It was from Dave, around midnight. He had texted earlier in the day asking about something work related, and she mentioned that she was being swept away by Liz and Sarah for the weekend. This time he sent just a simple smiley face. Margaret felt a little giddy.

The next morning came a few short hours later, but they couldn't wait to get ready and head out to soak up more of the city so nice, they named it twice. Sarah had snagged tickets to an Off-Broadway show that night and they wanted to spend the day visiting some museums. A cab delivered them Pier 61 where they boarded a luxury yacht for a brunch cruise on the Hudson River. With the spectacularly scenic views of the city skyline floating by, they sipped bottomless mimosas and once again ate like royalty. The food in NYC was out of this world.

"OK," Liz said, looking over the itinerary she'd made as they disembarked. "I say we head to the museum, grab lunch, go back to the room to relax and freshen up, go to the play, and then have a late dinner."

Margaret and Sarah were happy to have their own personal travel agent and tour guide in Liz. It sure made everything easier, and all of the surprise places were fun.

They grabbed another cab, this time to the Museum of Modern Art, where they opted for the headphone tour. At times, they separated to look at different things that interested them. Margaret felt so inspired by the beautiful paintings. She couldn't help but think of how amazing Dave's creations were. She felt they could easily be displayed in this museum. She sure was thinking about him an awful lot lately. It all felt too soon though. He was just a friend, after all.

They spent a couple hours at the MoMA, which still didn't feel like enough time to take everything in. The evening went by in fast-forward as well, once back to their room, they freshened up and relaxed for a bit before it was time to head off to their play. It was at a smaller theater, and they had seats right near the orchestra pit. The theater lights flashed a couple times, indicating the play was about to start, then dimmed. The spotlight turned on, the curtains opened, and they were transported to another world, a world of singing and dancing, laughter and tears. They were blown away by the exceptional performance.

It was 10 p.m. when the play let out, along with all the other shows in the Theatre District. They were starving and ready for dinner, so as people poured onto the street from every direction, Liz hailed a cab, and they were off to another surprise location. This time, they arrived at a fancy vegetarian restaurant. They weren't vegetarians per se, but loved vegetarian food nonetheless. This restaurant was modern and hip, with lounge music playing and eccentric, interesting dishes passed by in servers' hands as they were led to their table. Once they sat down, a terra-cotta pot full of baked bread with a side of honey butter was placed in front them.

The drink menu had the most interesting concoctions. Beet lemonade, carrot ginger cocktail, and homemade celery soda.

The food menu was even more diverse, and since they were starving, they ordered way too much. Three appetizers for the table, plus an entrée each. Wanting to try it all, they took bites off random plates and shared each other's meals—avocado stuffed with fried rice, rutabaga fondue, roasted golden beets, smoked trumpet mushrooms and tofu. The food was so flavorful, even meat eaters would love it, they concluded. For dessert, they shared a cake made with avocado cream cheese frosting. Sounded completely weird, granted, but they were assured by the server that it was delicious, and it was.

"I just want to thank you two for taking me away for the weekend. The last month or so has been pretty rough, but lately things are really starting to look up. This trip has rejuvenated me," Margaret said.

Liz and Sarah smiled.

"We are so glad to hear that. We just want you and the girls to be happy!" Liz said.

They were all completely exhausted from the many fun things they did that day. NYC definitely was not meant to be a relaxing getaway. Grabbing a cab back to the hotel, they called it a night, and thus the curtain fell on their whirlwind weekend. It felt too short and just right all at the same time. The next day they were heading back home, and as fun as the city was, there was always something great about going back to your own home in your small shore town, and especially your own bed. And Margaret definitely wasn't going to complain about getting back to the ocean-blue eyes that had begun to make her feel both like a new version of herself and the person that she used to be but had lost sight of long ago.

CHAPTER NINE

"Hey. Are you doing anything? I was wondering if you wanted to start doing some work together on the garden?" Dave asked after Margaret answered his phone call.

It was the first week of June already, and although Margaret had put hours and hours of work in on her favorite day of the year—planting day!—in her own garden at home, she was essentially running a few weeks behind with getting the new garden in at Liz and Greg's place.

"That sounds great. What are you thinking?"

"Well, how about I swing by and pick you up, and we can go buy flats of vegetable seedlings at the nursery. The girls are in school, right?"

"Yep. They are. That sounds great. I can be ready in half an hour. Just let me let Liz and Greg know that we're starting the garden, and ask my Mom if she can be at my house after school to stay with the girls, since I know this will go past 3 p.m."

"Perfect. Also, I'm grabbing a rototiller from my friend's house, and we'll start tilling the ground today. We should be able to get a lot of plants in. It's a little late in the growing season, but I think if we buy bigger seedlings and fertilize them, they'll catch right up soon."

Forty-five minutes later, Dave pulled up in his truck. The rototiller sat in the back with some other gardening tools, and he had tan overalls on, boots, and a backwards hat that made his thick wavy hair pop out on the sides a little.

Margaret laughed as she got into the truck. "So, you're really a farmer today, huh?"

Dave laughed. "Yep. From what I remember, rototilling can get pretty messy. I figured I'd better be prepared."

Dave flipped on the local classic rock radio station, and they were off to the garden center.

"I hope you don't mind, but my air conditioning bit the dust a couple weeks ago. It's getting fixed next week, but for now we'll keep the windows down."

Margaret laughed as the wind whipped her hair everywhere. She had forgotten to grab a hair tie. "It's totally fine. I love fresh air."

The hot sun warmed her arms and face, and the fresh air and music made her feel alive. Out of the corner of her eye, Dave glanced over at her with a smile on his face. Maybe he could feel the happiness radiating from her.

When they pulled up to the garden center, Dave immediately hopped out and opened Margaret's door before she'd had a chance to shove her bag closed and unbuckled her seat belt. She was not used to such attentive thoughtfulness.

"How have I never been to this place?" Margaret asked in awe as she stepped out of the truck.

"It's a place that we went to a lot when I was kid. It's been handed down from generation to generation. They don't really advertise, and it's off the beaten path since it's down that long dirt road, but they basically make a good business from word-of-mouth and their regulars."

There were hundreds of flats of flowers and vegetable seedlings and tons of greenhouses everywhere. Past the greenhouses, wide meadows of land spanned in every direction. A couple dogs greeted them as they walked up, allowing some scruffs behind the ears before they ran off noisily, disturbing a gray cat asleep in a small spot between a flat of geraniums and impatiens.

"Dave? Wow. How long has it been?" a man said, wiping his hands on a towel that hung from his back pocket.

"Years! Holy cow. How have you been, Chris?" Dave asked while shaking Chris's hand.

"We've been great. Business is good. Kids are good. I don't think I've seen you since we graduated," Chris said.

Dave looked over at Margaret. "This is my friend Margaret, her sister bought my parents' old property, as crazy as that is. Margaret and I work together, and I'm going to help them restore parts of the land. Today we're tilling and hoping to get some vegetable seedling plants in."

"How cool is that. I have some fond memories of that farm with you and your brothers growing up. If you need any help over there, let me know. I'd love to see that property looking good again. I drive past it a lot," Chris said.

Margaret smiled. "That would be awesome. We may take you up on that, Chris."

"We've got a ton of different vegetable plants available. My wife went crazy with the heirloom seeds, as well. Our customers have been loving the unique varieties. Those five greenhouses over there are all vegetables, and those five over there are flowers. Grab me when you're ready to pay and I'll give you my friends and family discount," Chris said with a wink.

Margaret clasped her hands together. "OK, now I'm really excited. I had a bunch of heirlooms in my garden at home before it was destroyed by the storm. I didn't have time to start them indoors again. I can't wait to look at them all."

They both grabbed pull carts and headed to the vegetables. Margaret started making flats up with different packs of tomatoes. She grabbed heirloom orange tomatoes, striped tomatoes, green tomatoes, purple tomatoes, and even blue ones. They had every variety under the sun: slicer tomatoes, cherry tomatoes, saladette tomatoes, and grape tomatoes. The options were endless. She was in her element. She also put two whole flats of red hybrid tomatoes on her cart. They were typically more disease resistant than the heirlooms, so she liked to plant those as well.

Dave was in the next row over, grabbing pepper plants. Bell peppers, banana peppers, jalapeños, sweet snacking peppers.

"Dave, this place is blowing me away. They have hundreds of varieties of tomatoes. All of the other places nearby sell maybe ten varieties of red tomatoes," Margaret said, looking at a nearby tomato name tag.

"I'm glad you like it. I've got plenty of room in the back of my truck for these flats. So, let's do it up. I was thinking we'll grab some bulk flower seeds for a wildflower garden and corn seeds for some cornfields, as well as some bags of compost for fertilizing, and straw for mulching. Heck, we should get cattle panels, too, for trellising the tomatoes and cucumbers and stuff. Gosh, we're definitely going to have to do multiple trips. We can get the rest of the it on our next free day."

"Oh, that's perfect. I was going to suggest most of those things, as I use it all every year in my garden," Margaret beamed.

Margaret usually did all these gardening tasks herself. She never had any help. Paul was not interested in the least. The girls "helped," but not really. They were too young to really put in too much effort. She had a small rototiller of her own, but it constantly had issues and it wiped her out after only a half hour of using it. She was glad to have someone willing to do the heavy work.

They paid for their items, talked to Chris and his wife one last time, and were off.

"Are you hungry? Want to stop somewhere to eat first

before we get to work?" Dave said as he shifted the truck into drive.

"I thought you'd never ask. I'm starving. I haven't eaten anything yet today."

"I know a great little oyster place that has outdoor seating overlooking the wetlands. They have other things besides oysters, but that's what everyone knows them for. It's a town over. What do you think?"

"That sounds great." Margaret was surprised she had never heard of the place. Then again, Paul didn't like seafood, so that's probably why. They were always trying to find somewhere to go out to eat that would appease both of them. Seafood restaurants were usually out of the question.

Fifteen minutes later, they pulled up to what amounted to a shack, for all intents and purposes, with open-air seating in the front.

The place was pretty busy for noon on a weekday. Almost every stool was occupied, and most of the patrons had a big tray of raw oysters on ice in front of them. Margaret and Dave were seated right away at a shaded table on the deck overlooking the water.

There were white egrets in the distance and multiple osprey nests with ospreys on them. A great blue heron was busy trying to catch its lunch, eventually spearing a fish and flipping it up to swallow it whole.

They looked over the menu. Dave already knew what he wanted—oysters, of course. Margaret opted for a crab cake sandwich with fries.

"You know, I have to say … it's been nice getting out of the house and starting this new project with you. Today has been a lot of fun already," Dave said, leaning back in his chair and stretching his arms behind his head.

Margaret smiled. "I was thinking the same thing. I've never really had someone to garden with, or even do a big project like this with, to be honest."

"Is that so? My ex hated gardening too. We lived on a small suburban lot for years, and I just didn't feel motivated to start a garden myself, so I never did. It always made me a little sad that I wasn't using everything I'd learned from growing up on a farm. Heck, she didn't even like to cook. I did most of the cooking in that house. She would have gone out to eat every day if she could have."

"I think our exes have a lot in common. Let that be a sign that we surely are better off now without them."

Margaret took a sip of her drink and looked out over the wetlands to see what looked like a bonded male and female swan.

"You see that? I read that swans mate for life a lot of times. That is pretty uncommon for the bird world," Margaret said, as the breeze lifted her hair up off her neck. She still hadn't taken her eyes off the swans but could definitely feel someone hadn't taken their eyes off of her. Those butterflies *whooshed* again in her stomach.

After lunch, they took off for the farm, riding down back dirt roads bordered by the marshes, marinas, farms, and the bay. Margaret found one of Dave's hats next to her and put it on to tame her hair. Dave looked over at her, a lingering glance with a contented smile, and then turned up the radio.

* * *

"Hey, Liz, we're here," Margaret said into the phone as they pulled up.

"You don't have to call me or ask to come here, you know," Liz said. "We want you use this land as though it's yours. We want you to feel like it's yours, even though we own it. Lord knows Greg and I won't be doing anything with all those acres. It'll just sit there."

"Well, thank you, Liz. I figured you'd want to hang out

with your sister and do some backbreaking work out here with Dave and I," Margaret joked.

"Maybe a little later on," Liz laughed. "I'm going to a client's house and Greg's working from home. You two enjoy yourselves."

Dave drove all the way to the back of the property and hopped out to grab Margaret's door again. Unused to such gestures, Margaret was just throwing it open as he walked up. "You don't have to open my door for me. We're equals." Margaret was accustomed to being a pretty independent woman.

"Oh, I know I don't *have* to. I just like to do it. If you don't want me to, I can stop."

Margaret blushed. "Well, if you like to do it, then you can continue. I guess I'm just not used to it."

Dave smiled warmly, his eyes never leaving hers. "Just look at it as a sign of respect."

Margaret nodded and smiled, releasing an appreciative sigh.

Dave hopped into the back of the truck, setting up a ramp to bring the rototiller out. "I'm going to start tilling the land here. I can make it pretty big, if you'd like. This thing is a beast. We can make multiple plots."

Margaret looked out towards the fields. The sun shone down brightly on everything, making it a perfect space for growing everything she wanted to grow.

"Well, I was thinking multiple plots would be great. We can do vegetables in one, then the vining crops, like the pumpkins and melons that end up taking over in their own plot, then another plot for wildflowers, and another for corn and sunflowers. Does that sound OK?" Margaret asked.

Dave gazed out over at the land, a satisfied look lit his eyes as he squinted against the sun's brilliant rays and a small smile tugged at his lips. "That sounds perfect. Do you want to start hoeing rows behind me as I till? That way we can double up and get ready for planting today. These vegetables need to get in the ground as soon as possible."

Though the sun beat down on them, they ended up working for hours preparing the soil. Margaret had packed a cooler full of drinks and snacks, and they had already drunk a ton between the two of them. Their shirts were soaked through with sweat and dirt and they smelled like sunblock, but it was the most content Margaret had felt in years.

After the first plot of land was tilled, Margaret grabbed bags of compost to mix into the rows that she'd hoed. Buying compost in bulk probably would have been better, but they didn't want to wait a week for delivery. Typically, Margaret made her own compost, but that would take time on this new property.

By dinnertime, they'd decided to call it a day. Dave had tilled all the plots and finished hoeing rows while Margaret planted. They had two plots completely done and planted.

"OK, I'm going to water these seedlings, and I think that will be good for today. We can store the tiller and the gardening tools in the garage. They made space for us," Margaret said, dragging a long hose.

Dave smiled. "That sounds perfect."

"So, I think I'm going to take the girls and my mom out for pizza in about an hour, after I get home and shower. You're more than welcome to come along."

Dave took his hat off and ran his fingers through his messy hair. "I might take you up on that. I'm starving as well, and I need to grocery shop. I'll drop you off, head home to shower, and meet you there—if that's alright."

"That sounds great. I think the girls will be excited to have company. We can discuss the garden with them. They love helping me in the garden so they may be out here with us pretty soon."

An hour later, Margaret, the girls, and Judy were seated a table at a local pizza place that Margaret loved. Ten minutes later, Dave walked in looking very different than she'd ever seen him before. He had on a button-down shirt, jeans that fit perfectly in all the right places, and leather boat shoes. He looked rather dressed up from how she normally saw him. He still looked just as attractive as he did when dirty and sweaty, just in a different way.

"Hi, Dave. This is my mother, Judy, and you've met my daughters, Abby and Harper, at Liz and Greg's," Margaret said getting up from her seat to greet him.

"Hello, everyone. I've heard a lot about you, Judy," he smiled, shaking her hand. "I hear you're an amazing mother, and Abby and Harper,"—he turned to the girls—"I hear you two love to garden. Did you want to help us start the new garden at your aunt and uncle's new house?"

Harper immediately piped up. "Yes, we definitely want to help. We love planting seeds. Not so much weeding, though."

Margaret and Judy laughed.

"Oh, that's totally fine. You can let me handle all that weeding. We will definitely need your help when we plant the corn and wildflower seeds. We could use the help of big strong girls like you two. Does that sound good?" Dave flexed his bicep to make them laugh.

Harper and Abby both nodded, giggling as their legs dangled side to side in their seats.

"OK, let's order already. We're starving," Judy said, studying the menu.

Margaret couldn't imagine having a better day than she'd had. Working on the farm felt so rewarding and fulfilling. Lunch had been amazing, and she now had this new friend in Dave, the guy at work who'd always kept to himself. The coworker she barely gotten to know in all these years—who knew that he'd turn out to be such a wonderful person? Now here he was, eating pizza with her mom and daughters, and by choice. He wanted to be here. She had only started getting to know him, but it actually felt like they had known each other for a long time. They had so much in common and saw Cape May, particularly the farm, through a shared lens.

Judy flagged down the server. "We'll have two plain pies, and a couple house salads with your house vinaigrette, please." Once the server walked off to put their order in, Judy looked over at Dave. "Why do you look so familiar to me?"

"Did you ever shop at the Piping Plover Farms stand years ago?" Dave asked.

"Why yes, I went there every week in the summer for those Jersey tomatoes and delicious homemade pies. I always stopped after work on my way home."

Margaret laughed. "Well, that explains why Liz and I had never heard of Piping Plover Farms. You always went without us."

Dave chimed in, "Well, that was my family's old farm. The property that Liz and Greg now own. Margaret and I were out there today getting it ready for a big garden. I'm sure she told you all about it already."

Margaret cleared her throat. "Yeah, I did tell you, didn't I?"

Judy rolled her eyes and laughed. "This one. She forgets to tell me a lot of things. I'll have to keep up through you now, Dave."

Judy and Paul were never close, no easy banter was had or lighthearted ribbing, and now here was Margaret's mom, already chummy with Dave. As much as Margaret loved her mother, she knew most people had to earn her approval, sometimes over many years. Yet here, in a matter of minutes, it looked like Dave already had.

CHAPTER TEN

The next day, Margaret called Joan and asked her supervisor if she could try and help with building donations back up again. Margaret loved her job and place of work. Not only did the Pine Tree Wildlife Refuge benefit wildlife in need, but also the community, and she wanted to help by volunteering a little extra time to get them back on their feet.

Joan was a little hesitant. "Well, you know we employ people to take care of that. I don't want to step on any toes. Eleanor has been in charge of that for thirty years now."

"Yes, but you know I have experience with fundraising from my last nonprofit job. We aren't doing any social media fundraising, and that is holding us back. The events that Eleanor puts together are great, but I don't think it's enough to keep up with donations needed these days." *Obviously.*

Eleanor was not up to speed on social media, admittedly having only used it a couple times when her grandchildren showed her. She much preferred to keep in touch with people via phone and e-mail. She was excellent at throwing events to raise money, but they were the same events, over and over, for the past thirty years from what Margaret had been told. She wasn't too keen on change in any form, and Margaret was pretty sure the puffy paint sweatshirt craft day with the kids was way too outdated.

"Well, I think you're onto something here. How about you take over the social media page? Gosh, nobody has posted on that thing in years. Last I checked, I think we had over seven thousand followers too. I'll let Eleanor know that I'm delegating this part of the fundraising to you. Just keep me updated."

* * *

A week went by and Margaret had decided to bring the girls to the farm to help plant the corn, sunflower, and wildflower seeds. Dave had tilled all the plots and everything else had been planted already. He had texted her earlier that he was planning to stop by to bring over the straw and cardboard for mulching the walkways and around the plants. This helped keep weeds out and kept the soil moist longer on hot days. Margaret had already told Liz and Greg that she would cover their next water bill, as it probably was going to be double with all the watering.

Dave pulled up twenty minutes later with a huge stack of hay bales tied down in the bed. He also had a bunch of long rolls of black tubing.

"Hey, Dave!" Abby and Harper yelled from the plot they were throwing wildflower seeds around on. They had loved Dave since the day they met him. Maybe it was the way he made them laugh or the way he included them in activities around the farm. They had only been around him a couple times but had asked about him a lot since.

Dave hopped out of the truck and yelled over to the girls. "Whatcha planting over there? The biggest, baddest wildflower garden around, I assume."

The girls laughed and continued with their planting. There

were many bags of seed to spread so they had their work cut out for them.

"Hey," Dave said as he turned his hat backwards.

Margaret had a thing for backwards hats on men. Particularly on Dave.

"Hey, yourself. I know what all the straw is for, but what are you doing with that black tubing?" Margaret asked while adding in T-posts for where she wanted the cattle panel trellising.

"Oh, that's for the drip irrigation system," Dave said looking over at it.

"You're kidding. I've always wanted drip irrigation."

Dave sighed, "Yeah, I figure we might as well get it in the ground now instead of waiting. It will save on water costs significantly, and it will allow for the leaves to not get wet as much, except for when it rains, of course."

Margaret looked at her watch. "Paul is coming to pick the girls up for dinner around five, so I probably can't stay too long today."

"Oh, well would you want to grab a bite to eat and do a little trail walking after he picks them up?" Dave said.

Margaret laughed. "That would be nice. Also, I'm pretty sure the girls will be jealous they can't come hang out with you." Dave furrowed his brow in a playful way, like he thought she was joking. "I'm dead serious. They can't stop talking about you. You've got a way with kids. Who knew?"

"Well then, we will definitely find time to spend with the girls. I have all sorts of fun things up my sleeve we can do with them. Do you want me to pick you up, say, around six?"

"That works for me. Gives me time to clean up."

* * *

Six o'clock rolled around, and when Dave pulled up to Margaret's driveway, she was waiting outside.

"Hop on in. Where did you want to eat?" Dave said joyfully.

"How about that little outdoor spot up the road. The one that has the pretty market lights over the tables?" Margaret said.

"Oh yeah, The Blue Swan. Great food, and not too far from the trails."

After arriving and ordering drinks and food, Margaret spilled the beans about work.

"So, last week I asked Joan if I could volunteer with raising donations since I have experience doing it with my last job. I am a little rusty, it's been years, but I remember a lot and I keep up with what's new and hip. Having two young girls obsessed with every new app helps with that. Joan gave me the reins to the social media sites. A friend of mine runs a nonprofit and they started ramping up their social media donation links and keeping the page active with creating fundraising events and so forth, and they have nearly doubled their donations."

"You're kidding. How has it been going so far?" Dave asked.

"Well, I coordinated with Eleanor and created a ton of events on the social media page for everything that's coming up at the refuge. Already, thousands of people have clicked the interested button and shared the post. I've seen the follower count on the page go up by hundreds since I added those. Then, I started sharing some posts to our followers, filling them in on the hard times the refuge is going through with the drop-in donations, and how important donations are. I added a donate button, and we are already up to five-thousand dollars in donations in only two days. I've been taking tips from my friend for what works at her nonprofit, and it's working amazingly well. I have a ton more things I need to get done, though. I've been using my extra free time to do it."

"Impressive, Margaret. I'm really glad you stepped up to

make this happen. The refuge has been struggling for years now, but this year has been the worst, obviously," Dave said shaking his head.

"Yeah, I think everyone is stuck in their old ways there and it's holding them back. I think I can help bring in more donations than they've ever received," Margaret said optimistically.

They finished their meals and drinks and got back into the truck, headed for a trail walk at Cape May Meadows.

They pulled into the gravel parking lot and hopped out. It was already dusk, and the grasses in the meadows were high all around the trail. The trail itself lead through wetlands and to the beach, with stopping points for bird watching. There were egrets and lots of Canada geese hanging out in the water. They quietly walked the trails, taking in the sights and nature sounds. It was a peaceful way to spend the evening, walking in nature with someone who held the same appreciation for it.

"Hey, I have to pick up some olive oil at the outdoor mall. Do you want to tag along? I won't be long," Dave said as they walked back to the truck.

"Sure. Paul said he'd have the girls back at nine, so we have about an hour until I have to be back."

The outdoor mall was just a section of town with mostly little mom-and-pop shops, one after another, on a brick walkway spanning about three blocks. There were fountains and benches and restaurants with outdoor seating. It was a pretty happening spot in town, especially on summer nights.

"I'm going to get some fudge over there while you grab your olive oil, and we can meet up by the fountain. Does that work?" Margaret asked.

"Sounds perfect. See you in about ten minutes." Dave took off in the other direction.

Margaret impulsively turned back to look at Dave over her shoulder, and it gave her a little jolt to find that he had done the same and was already looking back at her. Margaret's cheeks flushed and her heart fluttered. *He's just a friend, Margaret.*

Ten minutes later, after meeting up in front of the fountain, they strolled the shops, popping into one known for having every scented type of bar soap one's heart desired. The floral smell of the store hit hard at first, and then mellowed out after a minute or so of getting used to it. They had lavender soaps, oatmeal soaps, rose soaps, pumpkin soaps, pine tree soaps—everything! Margaret found a section of beautifully packaged soaps from France. She dragged her hand gently down the row of them until she got to an interesting one labeled Ice Cream. She lifted it to her nose and took a deep breath, inhaling the slightly muted scent. It smelled just like a vanilla ice cream cone. It took her instantly back to being a kid on the beach. She and Liz would screech with excitement whenever the ice cream man rang his bell at their beach entrance. They would scramble for money from their parents and race over to grab their favorite frozen treat.

Margaret held the soap up to show Dave, who was across the room smelling more manly scents. "This is the one. I have to have it," Margaret said enthusiastically.

Dave smiled and held up a whole basket of soaps. "I'm getting all of these."

After paying, and just as they were stepping out of the store, Abby and Harper ran over to them out of nowhere.

"Hi, Mom! Hi, Dave!"

"Hi, girls. What are you doing here? Where's your father?" Margaret asked, a little concerned.

"He's over there. He gave us some money to grab ice cream and we saw you!" Abby said as that very ice cream dripped down her arm.

Margaret and Dave both looked over to where Abby pointed.

"Who is he with? Oh, I see. It's good ole Sandy," Margaret said sarcastically out of the corner of her mouth to Dave.

"They brought some friends with them to dinner tonight.

They're over there," Harper said, taking a lick of her chocolate ice cream.

"Wait. Is that Will? Your dad's work friend?" Margaret asked out loud, though she was talking more to herself than the girls.

"That's Will and Michelle," Dave confirmed quietly to Margaret so the girls wouldn't hear.

Margaret's eyes widened. "You've got to be kidding me. How small *is* Cape May?" she whispered.

Dave sighed then chuckled. "Pretty small, I guess."

"Alright girls, your father is supposed to drop you off back at home soon, and since we're here, I'm going to ask him if we can just take you now. Let's walk over there and talk to him."

It was awkward the moment they all saw each other. Everyone gave cordial hellos without looking at one another too long. The silence in the air was deafening.

Dave tried to crack an awkward joke to break the tension. "Well, look at us all here together like one big family."

Everyone kind of fake laughed. *He tried.*

Sandy and Michelle whispered to each other, snickering. Margaret's blood started to boil. She looked to Paul who was staring at his phone.

"So, how long have you all known each other?" Margaret asked out of spite.

Sandy grabbed Paul's arm aggressively and whispered something in his ear. He just nodded.

"Since recently, aside from Will," Paul said, still not looking at Margaret.

Margaret knew immediately that Sandy had whispered instructions for him to lie. The e-mails were proof. She definitely had some kind of control over him. To think he ruined their marriage over this woman. Is this what he wanted? Someone who had control over him? Then again, their marriage was going downhill prior to all of this anyway. Margaret knew the divorce was for the best but couldn't help but be angry. She wanted to ask more questions. Maybe hint at the fact that she knew he was lying. The girls were there though. This wasn't the time or place. Maybe it never would be or should be. She needed to move on for good.

"Well, look at the time. I guess we ought to be going," Dave said, knowing full well the conversation was about to take a turn for the worse.

Margaret piped in, "Hey, Paul. I'm thinking we might as well take the girls home since we're here."

Abby and Harper, clueless about the awkwardness and what was going on, jumped up and down. "Yes! We love riding in Dave's truck."

They couldn't get away fast enough, and as soon as they were out of their exes' earshot, Dave said, "I've run into Will and Michelle multiple times over the past year. I'm sort of used to it now. We say hi, and that's it. I have nothing more to say to them. It was a rough divorce, but I've come out a better man. I try to look at the positive. I'm always here to listen and give advice while you go through yours," Dave said.

Margaret smiled. "Thank you, Dave. That means a lot."

As Margaret, Dave, and the girls walked towards the truck, Dave gently put his hand on Margaret's back. She felt a *whoosh* sweep over her. She had never really felt his touch before, and this very moment couldn't have been a more perfect time.

CHAPTER ELEVEN

It was the week of Fourth of July, and the entire family was parked outside of Aunt Mary's Cape May B&B, unloading their luggage on a hot, foggy morning. Judy had arrived first and stood on the steps greeting and directing everyone while Bob relaxed in one of the many rocking chairs on the huge wraparound porch. He was a simple man and didn't want to be too involved. He would rather listen to the baseball game on the old radio.

Aunts, uncles, and cousins, both somewhat local and from all over the country, showed up. There was thirty of them total, including many of the cousins' kids, some of them the same age as Abby and Harper.

Days prior, Judy, Margaret, and Liz had put fresh linens on the beds and tidied up the place since the B&B wasn't being regularly used and cleaned. Margaret had cut some fresh flowers out of her yard and placed them in vases around the house. Liz had baked a ton of pies and stacked them up neatly in boxes on the kitchen table.

The steps up to the place were a little steep, so the men brought most of the luggage to the rooms while the women made their way around to see the spectacular B&B on the beach.

It was fun to see everyone's jaw drop at the beauty of the place, even from the moment they pulled up and realized *this* was *the* place they were staying at.

After everyone got settled in, Margaret and Liz whipped up some snacks since people were hungry from their long drive and plane ride. Margaret made a huge cheese board and Liz made a few of her famous dips, her spinach bread bowl dip being one of Margaret's favorites. As expected, the entire family devoured the food. That made Margaret and Liz happy. They loved feeding people.

While Judy and her siblings made their way to the back porch for some catching up, the kids put their swimsuits on, ready to spend hours playing in the pool. Margaret and Liz gathered with their female cousins on the deck to catch up and chat while keeping an eye on the kids. The men huddled out front, standing by the cars, passing around cigars and talking.

The way they did these vacations every year was the same. Since there were thirty of them, it was a little hard to go out to dinner. They usually did that once, on Monday night with a reservation. For the other days of the week, they made a chart of who cooked what when. Aunt Debbie always did a Sunday night barbeque. She made the best homemade baked beans and would never share the recipe. Uncle Phil usually made his specialty, fried chicken with all the sides, on Tuesday. Margaret and Liz did brunch together on Wednesday morning, and so on. It was a fun little system that the aunts and uncles put together ages ago when the yearly reunion first started.

"Hey, everyone!" Sarah said as she walked out onto the deck.

"Sarah!" everyone yelled as they got up to give her big hugs.

Margaret and Liz invited Sarah to their family reunion

every year. Usually, she would drive up to the Poconos for a few days. Everyone loved her and considered her part of the family, having known her for many years from when Margaret and Liz brought her to the weekly vacations as kids. It was fun to see how close Sarah had gotten to some of the aunts, uncles, and cousins. She became social media friends with a lot of them, and they kept close that way.

Everyone asked about Paul and where he was, and Margaret found herself telling the same story about twenty times. She didn't like that part. She felt that they were pitying her, but she wanted to look at change as something positive. A fresh start on life. She thought about what Dave said about being positive about it, and it really resonated with her.

Dinner rolled around. The first night of vacation was always pizza delivery day. They had a ton of different pizzas and salads delivered to the house. The kids especially loved this dinner day. Everyone spread out on the deck, porch, and dining room table to eat.

Margaret's extended family had been scattered growing up. She loved this big, giant family and the week they spent together. It made her happy to be around all of them at once.

After dinner, as Margaret and Liz were helping clean up all the paper plates, napkins, and pizza boxes, Margaret bit her lip and looked over at Liz.

"What? I know that look. What are you thinking?" Liz asked.

"Should I invite Dave to stop by? Is it too soon, since I just told everyone about Paul? I mean he's just a friend, so it's not like I'm introducing my new boyfriend. He's really been helping me with the divorce and the new garden, and the girls absolutely love him and would be thrilled to have him come. I'm just worried about what everyone will think."

"Well, you did mention to everyone that your friend Dave was helping you with the new garden, right? I think it's fair to say that they will probably enjoy meeting him. Plus, this is your family. They don't give a hoot about Paul. They want you to be happy."

"You're right. I'm going to invite him," Margaret said grabbing her phone to send a text.

Hey, Dave. We are having our family reunion at my aunt's place on Beach Ave. at The Seahorse Inn. Here for the week if you'd like to stop by. The girls would love it, and I'm sure my big family would love to meet the friend that's helping me out with the new garden on Liz and Greg's property. They love the story of how we found out it used to belong to your family.

Dave immediately texted back.

That sounds great. I'm off the next couple of days. You guys doing the beach tomorrow? I can meet you there.

Yes! Family beach day tomorrow around 10 a.m. Bring a change of clothes so you can join us for my Aunt Debbie's amazing BBQ dinner later on.

* * *

The next morning, everyone did their own thing for breakfast. Some of the aunts and uncles went out together for a sunrise breakfast, others made eggs, and the kids mostly had bagels or a bowl of cereal. The great thing about these family vacations was that during the day, everyone kind of did their own thing so they weren't tethered to a schedule, and dinner time and after was the family time. However, beach day was going to be a whole-family affair.

By 10 a.m., all thirty of them had walked out front to the beach and plopped their stuff down right by the lifeguard station so they could keep an eye on the kids in the ocean. They had tons of umbrellas, canopies, coolers, boogie boards, and sand toys. A bunch of the guys brought games, as they couldn't sit still in the chairs all day. They ended up getting a pretty serious game of cornhole going that got strangers from all over the beach involved.

Uncle Phil put a big flag with an ocean scene in the sand so their little camp on the beach was easily found by others looking for them. Liz had packed a ton of sandwiches and snacks, and their Uncle Jack brought the old stereo. The stations down the shore hadn't changed what they played since Margaret graduated high school. That was part of the beauty of the Jersey shore—nostalgic songs on the beach that brought you back to the good ole times.

After getting settled in, Margaret felt a tap on her shoulder. She looked up to find Dave standing there, chair in one hand and a bag in the other.

Before Margaret could get a word out, Abby and Harper stopped what they were doing and ran over to him. "Dave! Dave! Look what we're making!" the girls chortled, pointing to a big sandcastle they were building with their cousins.

"Whoa, that's amazing. I'll have to show you how to make a drizzle castle when you're done. It's what we beach babies did as kids around these parts," Dave told them.

Margaret laughed. "Hey, plop your chair and stuff right here."

Greg immediately got up to shake Dave's hand and grab his bag for him so it didn't get full of sand just yet.

Margaret stood up and made a big announcement to the family. "Attention! Attention! This is my friend Dave I told you all about. He's helping build up our garden at Liz and Greg's. It was his family's old property."

"Oh, that's right. So nice to see you, Dave," Aunt Linda said.

"Yes, come hang out with the family. We're not yelling. We just talk loud," said Uncle Bill.

Everyone else waved and said hi before resuming their beach activity.

Later, after some relaxation, Margaret realized she could

only see Harper and not Abby. She jumped out of her chair and surveyed the ocean, looking for a glimpse of her.

Harper had run off to swim in front of the lifeguards with her cousins, but Margaret still couldn't see Abby.

"Hey! Does anyone see Abby?" Margaret asked starting to grow frantic.

"She was helping me build the sandcastle, and she walked to the ocean with her bucket to put water in it. We were trying to add a moat. She didn't come back. I figured she went swimming," said Marcus, her cousin's nine-year-old son.

"Oh no." Margaret put her hand to her mouth.

As the family collectively surveyed the beach, some stood out of their chairs to get a better look, others turned in circles, looking in all directions.

Dave sprang up out of his chair. "Marcus, which direction did you see her go in?"

Marcus pointed to the left, where you could see never-ending miles of beach with hundreds of beach chairs and umbrellas just like theirs. Everything must look the same to a six-year-old out here.

Before Margaret could say anything, Dave took off down the beach. Margaret shot off to walk to the other end of the beach. Everyone else stayed back to search locally, in case she came back on her own.

Margaret walked what felt like a half a mile, growing more worried by the minute. How had she gotten so far away? How had she slipped from Margaret's, and everyone else's, view so quickly?

Margaret turned around, heading back. She had left her cell phone in her bag by the chair and wasn't able to get any updates. The fog from the morning had come back over the beach, making visibility even worse. Her anxiety caused her stomach to knot as thoughts turned, unbidden, to all the worst scenarios. She'd experienced a traumatizing incident on the beach when she was eight, having been lost for a short time herself.

Through the fog, she made out Dave walking towards her. Holding his hand was Abby. She was crying and looked visibly upset. With a big wave of relief, Margaret ran towards them. She knelt down in front of Abby and cupped her face in her hands.

"You scared us half to death. Where were you? Did Dave find you?"

Dave, with sweat pouring down his face, looked nearly as relieved as Margaret felt.

Abby still had tears streaming down face. "I went to the ocean to grab a bucket of water and got lost."

Dave knelt down in front of Abby next to Margaret, "I found her sitting on the lifeguard stand with the lifeguards five blocks down. She was smart enough to tell them she was lost, but she couldn't remember your cell phone number. You know, smart phones these days and no one needing to know numbers like we did when we were kids …"

"Oh, well, I will definitely make sure my girls memorize my number from here on out. Let's get back to everyone else. They are also very worried."

She went to grab Abby's hand, but noticed she was already holding Dave's hand. She grabbed Abby's other hand, and they all walked along the beach together holding hands. Margaret looked over at Dave and they exchanged relieved smiles. "*Thank you,*" Margaret silently mouthed.

As predicted, everyone was standing up, nervously awaiting their arrival as they walked back. Concerned aunts, uncles, and cousins all wanted the scoop from Abby. Abby felt like she had been on the scary adventure of a lifetime and was excited to recount her experience to everyone. All of her cousins gathered around to hear it. This story was definitely going to be told for years to come.

Harper tugged on Dave's arm. "Let's do that drizzle castle you were talking about!"

All of the young cousins now surrounded Dave, waiting for him to show them this type of sandcastle they had never heard of.

Dave walked over to a clear spot of sand. "OK, well we need a few of buckets of water, but I'm going to be watching each and every one of you to make sure no one gets lost!"

The kids brought over the buckets of water, and Dave started filling them with sand. "Now watch me. You want the wet sand in the buckets to be able to drizzle out of your hands as it stacks up, like this."

The kids were in awe. How had they never thought of this?

Margaret sprawled out in her chair, getting comfortable next to Sarah and Liz. Watching Dave with the kids made her heart feel all warm and gooey. She kept feeling all these things that she hadn't felt in years, and it was both exciting and scary.

Margaret went into her bag to grab her phone to take a photo of the kids, and saw she had a missed call from Joan.

"That's weird. Joan just called me. She knows I'm on vacation this week," Margaret said to Sarah and Liz.

Although she'd really rather not return a work call while on vacation, Margaret got up to walk towards the dunes for privacy and quiet.

"Hey, Joan. How are you? I'm just returning your call."

"Oh Margaret, I have wonderful news. Whatever you have done to help with donations has worked. Eleanor said you raised a ton. In fact, it's more than we've seen in years for this quarter of the year. The wildlife refuge is finally getting to a good place again."

"Oh, that's wonderful!" Margaret said. She knew the social media donations were working, but hadn't checked on the progress since before vacation started.

"There is something I have to ask you though. Eleanor and I discussed this, and we were wondering if you would like a promotion to donations and fundraising?" She will probably be retiring soon, and we could really use your help in that department. You will get a small raise and can work from home if you want."

"Oh, goodness. What about the hospital? Who will manage that? I feel so connected to the animals and volunteers, and I don't know if I want to give that up," Margaret said.

"Well, that's up to you. If you wanted to divide up the days to a work a couple at the hospital and the others with donations, we could probably work that out. However, Rachel the intern has been here at the center all year and knows the place like the back of her hand. She would fit the manager role nicely with some extra training from you. If you didn't want to divide up your schedule, you could even come volunteer one night a week at the hospital, or pop in and visit whenever you wanted. There's definitely ways to still be connected."

Margaret thought about it. She liked the idea of working from home and having a raise. It would give her more freedom and perhaps more time to be with the girls and to work on other things like the garden. She wouldn't need her mom to stay with the girls after school anymore, but Judy probably would still want to come over. But what about Dave? Would they still stay connected? Well, that was a given. They'd been connected all this time during the cutbacks, so that wasn't anything to worry about. Could she make her own hours? If so, then this was a done deal.

"What are we thinking my hours would be?" Margaret asked.

"Well, that's also up to you. We just ask that you put in a forty-hour week. If you want to work four ten-hour days, that's fine. If you want to work five eight-hour days, that's also fine. Working from home will give you lots of flexibility. So, what do you think?" Joan asked eagerly.

"I think I'm going to take it. I will just help out at the hospital when I have free time and am missing being there. I'm really excited about this. Say, do you happen to know if everyone got their hours back?"

"Yep. Everyone's hours have been restored. We are excited to see what you and Eleanor and can do together!"

Margaret breathed a sigh of relief—Dave had his hours back too.

CHAPTER TWELVE

"How about we set up some decking here in the field between the gardens? I can build a pergola over it for shade. We could add some tables and chairs and white string lights. It would be a nice spot for a reprieve from the sun, a place to have lunches and drink morning coffee," Dave said as they walked around the beautiful garden, marveling at everything they had done.

"Are you serious? You could do that? That would be absolutely amazing," Margaret said, looking over at the girls who were harvesting baskets of zucchini and cucumbers with Liz's boys.

"Definitely. I'm done fixing up the house on the refuge, and I need more projects. I can get all the supplies for free or super cheap. Chris said he'd love to help me. I'm pretty excited to do it, actually. I have some other ideas, too ..."

On a Saturday in late July, Margaret marveled at the garden they had put in together. Huge and thriving, it was full of summer squash, tomatoes, cucumbers, eggplant, and peppers ready to harvest. There was so much of everything that they didn't know what to do with it all.

As they walked toward the tree line where the old chicken coops were, Margaret smiled. "Hey, I thought I should tell you.

I got the divorce papers today. The court signed off, and it's officially official. I'm so glad to have it over with. I can put it behind me now and move forward."

"You've already been moving forward." Dave reached over to pull a small leaf out of her hair.

Margaret blushed. "Thanks, Dave. You've been the most amazing friend through all of this. Working on this garden with you has brought new life to my soul. It gave me something to work towards and be happy about when everything else around me felt like it was crashing down. This garden saved me. It saved the old me that got lost somewhere in that marriage. I had to find her again, and I did."

Dave smiled. "I'm happy I could help you. I think being here at my old farm has helped me somehow, as well."

They walked until they stood in front of the run-down chicken coops.

"What do you think about these old chicken coops? Can they be salvaged? Would we have to build completely new ones?" Margaret asked.

Dave walked up close to the chicken coops to study them. "Oh, I'm going to build new ones, if that's alright. These haven't been touched in twenty-something years. They are completely rotted, and all the ivy and overgrowth on them hasn't helped. Are you sure we can do all this? Liz and Greg don't mind?"

"Nope. They actually love that we're doing this. They said to do whatever we want, as long as all permits are taken care of with the county. I just want to make sure we're not doing anything that's raising their property taxes too much. Of course, I would pay the difference."

Dave nodded and pointed out into the forest. "I wanted to show you something. It's way back in the trees though. It may not be there anymore. But I just need to see if it is. I think the kids will love it. They should probably tag along."

Margaret called for the kids, and they dropped their baskets and ran over.

They walked for a solid ten minutes through some thick overgrown brush, stepping over fallen tree limbs along the way, until they came to a creek. It was small, but mighty. It had lush green grass and moss on either side of it, and it made the most soothing sound. There was a sun beam shining down on it through the cracks of the trees. The kids shrieked and ran over to it, splashing their hands in to touch the cool water.

"It's our secret babbling brook!" Harper yelled out.

Dave laughed. "Yep. It was our secret little place as kids growing up too. It always felt like this mystical little spot that nobody knew about it. We played here for hours as kids."

Margaret looked over and saw something up in the trees. "What's that?"

"You've got to be kidding me. I can't believe it's still partly there. That's the remnants of the tree house we built as kids. Our dad helped us. We put it there so we could see our stream and watch all the animals that came by. We would read books and bring our radio and listen to the ball games up there. As teenagers, when one of us needed time alone or to escape, we had this tree house here," Dave said smiling.

The kids were astounded. "A real tree house? I thought they only existed in movies. I've never actually seen a real one, just those ones that are part of the jungle gyms, but they don't count," Liz's son, Michael, said.

"Yep. We had chairs and blankets up there. We tacked posters on the wall and had battery-operated lights. We even screened in the windows and door so bugs wouldn't get us. They can be awful out here during certain times of the year. Maybe I can rebuild it for you kids, but it would be a lot lower to the ground and much safer this time. I don't want anyone getting hurt."

The kids all shrieked in excitement, jumping up and down. Margaret knew her kids would want to be here all the time now. They loved the feeling of adventure and using their imagination.

"OK, let's head back. You kids can continue harvesting. We're going to walk around the property some more," Margaret said.

They walked over to the old run-down farm stand. Dave inspected what remained. "Well, some of the wood on this is still good. It just needs some refurbishing. I think with Chris's help, my brother and I can restore this beautifully. All of our extra produce could be sold in it with whatever else you wanted."

Margaret let out a sigh. "It has always been a dream of mine to run my own farm stand with what I grew. But do you think running it will be too much work with my full-time job?"

"Well, when my family ran their stand, it was small and manageable, like this one will be. You can make your own hours to work around your schedule, or do an honor system where people take what they want and leave money in a box. A lot of smaller stands around here do that. I can also help you run it, and I'm sure other friends and family members might like to chip in a few hours a week," Dave said with optimism in his voice.

Margaret felt her heart flutter with excitement. "You're right. There's a little stand near me that does the honor system. I've talked to them a few times, and it seems they do pretty well with it. I totally forgot about that."

"Hey, you know what? I forgot I have to pick something up at the store, and I think they close soon. I can be back here in about twenty minutes," Dave said, hurrying over to his truck.

The sun was about to set, and Margaret looked over again at the kids. They were now chasing each other all over the farm.

Her phone buzzed with a text alert from Liz.

Hey. Taking the boys out to get some food. Are you and Dave busy?

How about I take the girls with us? We might hit the shops after. It will give you and Dave some nice alone time. Hint, hint.

Margaret felt her cheeks blush.

They would love that. Thank you. Just let me know when you'll be back. Also, he's just a friend!

Liz was Team Dave all the way. Everyone was. Margaret knew it, but like she told everyone, he was just a friend. She was going through a divorce. He was recently divorced. Plus, she really enjoyed having him as a friend and was scared to lose that. He had pulled her through a dark period, and she had so much fun with him to boot.

Twenty minutes later, Dave pulled up in his truck and walked back over to Margaret, who still stood picturing what the farm market would be like.

"So, Liz and Greg are taking all of the kids out to dinner to let us finish up out here ...." Margaret looked over at the beautiful sunset starting to appear.

Dave ran his fingers through his hair, looking a little nervous. "I was thinking I'd like to walk over to Sunset Beach. I haven't been there in years. Wanna go?"

"Sounds great. I am getting a little hungry though. Maybe we can figure that out afterwards."

Dave smiled. "Yes, definitely."

The walk to Sunset Beach featured marshlands on their left with the beach straight ahead, about a seven-minute walk. The summer sounds of bugs, frogs, and birds filled the air and only an occasional car passed by. Their walk held an awkward silence that Margaret wasn't used to. Usually, they were always talking when they were together. Straight ahead, the sunset was just starting to slip below the horizon.

They walked past beautiful vineyards owned by the winery nearby and some horse farms with the most beautiful horses. There was an outdoor ring near the road that had trotting beams and jumps set up for those who took horseback riding lessons there, something Margaret would love to do again.

She loved Sunset Beach, even if it was a bit touristy. It was great that they could walk, because finding a parking spot wasn't easy in July. The beach was known for having the best sunsets around. People came from all over to collect Cape May diamonds, pure quartz crystals that looked like clear little pebbles within the sand. When polished and cut, they looked like real diamonds, hence the name.

They finally arrived at the beach, and Dave pointed to a spot to the right past where the crowds were. "Let's go over there, away from everyone, if that's OK."

Walking between all of the people who had set up their beach stations for the sunset, they dodged chairs set up with blankets and kids running to the water to splash their feet or look at all the horseshoe crabs that had been pushed to the water's edge, while their parents relaxed. Next door at the little restaurant on the beach, people ate their meals on the deck while joyfully chatting and watching the sunset. A few fishermen had their rods casted out, and others were combing the beach for shells. The water was calm, as was usual on the Delaware Bay side, with just some soft little waves lapping at the edge.

After a bit of walking, they were past everyone else and all by themselves on a piece of beach right up against the dunes. Margaret saw a blanket set up with the most beautiful spread of food. There were fresh grapes, some cut-up cheese, crackers, and bowl of strawberries. Two beautiful throw pillows were on the blanket, as well as a bouquet of flowers wrapped in newspaper. There was a little radio playing soft oldies songs next to the blanket.

"Well, this is just adorable, but who does it belong to? I don't see anyone around," Margaret said, looking up and down the beach.

Dave walked over to the blanket and sat down with his elbow propped on one of the throw pillows. "Here. Come sit with me."

"Is this yours? You set this up?" Margaret's eyes went wide with realization at the same time her pulse jumped.

"This is all mine. I set it up when I left the farm to go to the *store,"* Dave said, smiling.

"I don't know what to say, Dave. This is quite a surprise." A warm and fuzzy flush zipped from head to toe. Had Dave had feelings for her all along? Had they felt the same attraction towards each other all this time?

Margaret sat next to him on the blanket, undoing her sandals so she could dig her feet into the soft, cool sand. Dave did the same with his shoes. There was still a little bit of lingering quiet between them, aside from the soft music on the radio.

The sun disappeared further behind the horizon line, and the sky was turning hues of bright orange. Out in the distance, they could see the shipwreck in the water with birds perched atop it. It had been there since 1926. It sure gave a unique view for a sunset.

Margaret grabbed some grapes and cheese and felt a wave of happiness.

"Wait. Did you tell my sister you were doing this? Is that why Liz offered to take the kids out to eat?"

Dave laughed. "I did. I wanted to celebrate the finalization of your divorce. I know what a big day that is. It can be both happy and sad, and I wanted you to only remember it as happy."

Margaret grabbed his hand and squeezed. Her eyes welled up a little. "That is so sweet and thoughtful, Dave."

"And there's something else I have to add," Dave said looking straight at the sunset but still holding her hand.

"Yes?" Margaret said blotting her eyes.

"What would you say if I asked you to go to dinner with me?" he said, turning to her.

"Well, we've eaten dinner together a bunch already. I see no problem with it," Margaret said with a knowing smile.

"Well, I'm talking about something along the lines of a formal date," he clarified with a nervous smile.

Every hair on Margaret's arms raised, and in that second, it felt like they were the only people on the beach. The sky was now a purple-pink color, the sun having completely set, and perfectly on cue, the radio started playing the most romantic slow oldies song around.

"How could I say no to that?" Margaret said, laughing. "Of course I will."

Everyone else on the beach had packed up and scurried off, the sun's grand finale having concluded, and they found they were the only ones left.

"We could just stay out here and look at the stars next if you want," Dave said, half-serious. "Or, you know, we can hop in my truck, roll the windows down and take a ride among them all."

And in that moment, Margaret breathed a deep sigh of relief. Life sure had a funny way of working out, especially in Cape May.

EPILOGUE

October came fast, autumn having barreled in full force. There was a nice crispness to the air and the leaves had started to change color. Cape May was now a quieter beach town with the summer visitors mostly gone. Margaret and Dave had begun ripping up the diseased and dead parts of the garden in late August, replacing them with fall crops. Most of those were now ready for harvest. Carrots of every color, French breakfast radishes, kale, lettuce, peas so tasty that they tasted like candy right out of the pod, red and golden beets, broccoli, cauliflower, and plenty of pumpkins and gourds. Autumn was Margaret's favorite season, and she wanted every variety of pumpkin she could get: Jack-o'-lantern pumpkins, blue pumpkins, sugar pie pumpkins, mini pumpkins, white ghost pumpkins, all of them.

They finally got the farm stand up and running just in time to sell the fall harvest. Margaret stacked a beautiful display of pumpkins at the front of the stand and decorated the outside for the fall season with straw bales, mums, and corn stalks. All for sale, of course. Inside the stand, stood everyone helping get it ready for the farm stand's first day open.

Liz had made a batch of pies and boxed them up to be sold; Judy had made apple cider donuts; Sarah had knitted a bunch of hats and scarves; and Margaret had created little containers of her famous homemade egg salad, lavender lemonade, and jams, among many other things. The fall harvest was laid out beautifully in labeled wooden boxes. Even the kids made drawings that they wanted to contribute towards items for sale, which was adorable.

Dave and Greg perched on ladders together at the front, trying to hang the sign. It was a big wooden sign Dave and Margaret had made together, that had the name of the stand on it—*The Cape May Garden.*

It didn't take long to figure out a name for the stand. Dave and Margaret always referred to the whole area of crops and beds in general as "the garden" and it was in Cape May, and so a name was born.

The entire family helped hang the string market and twinkle lights from the ceiling inside. It gave everything such a warm glow. Margaret thrifted a bunch of ceramic Halloween pumpkins that she placed by the cash register. It had really come together.

Finally, it was ready for customers. Margaret made a social media page for it and posted in some local social media groups with photos of the new stand, which prompted a lot of interest.

* * *

By the next morning, many customers had already arrived. Liz offered to do the cash register that day, and Margaret and Dave focused on restocking items and adding some finishing touches.

By 6 p.m., they'd tidied up the place and closed up shop. The whole family was giddy with excitement to have all worked on something successful together.

"OK, time for a celebratory dinner. I'm ordering pizzas

and salads for everyone," Liz announced to the entire family as they finished up.

The kids screamed in happiness and the rest of the family walked back to the house.

"This place is beautiful. I can't thank you enough," Margaret said to Dave as they stood out front, arms around each other's backs, admiring the beautiful farm stand they had put together themselves.

"I have to say, I'm feeling a little nostalgic looking at it. It's even more beautiful than the one that was originally here when I lived here. My parents would be thrilled to see this," Dave said.

"When will your parents visit Cape May again?" Margaret asked

"Well, since they moved to Florida, they always want us to visit them, not vice versa. They rarely come back to Jersey, but they did say that they want to come up for Christmas this year. I'm pretty excited for them to meet you and the girls and see the farm. However, fair warning—my mom can be a little direct …."

Margaret smiled. "Oh, that would be lovely. I can't wait to meet them."

"I think most of my out-of-state siblings and their families are coming into town too. It will be the first time everyone has gotten together in years. I'm actually pretty excited, though it's a shame the stand will be closed up for the winter season and the garden will be gone when they get here. I'm really going to push for them to come visit next summer so they can see all of the work we've done."

"Cape May is a beautiful in the winter, especially during Christmas. I have a feeling it will be quite magical in its own way. Maybe we can do a toasty bonfire with hot cocoa and big warm wool blankets," Margaret suggested.

"Oh, that does sound rather nice. I used to hate winter, but the older I get, the more I appreciate it for what it is. If it snows, we could have the kids build snowmen out here, go sledding on the hill on the other side of the property. OK, now I'm getting excited," Dave said with his eyes glowing like a little kid's.

"Well, let me go grab my stuff, and we can head in to dinner with everyone," Margaret said, reaching for her purse. "That's weird," she murmured, looking at her phone.

"What?" Dave asked.

"My Aunt Mary just called. I haven't talked to her in a couple months."

Dave thought for a second. "The Aunt Mary who owns the B&B on the beach?"

"Yep. There's a message. Let me see what she wants," Margaret said as she held the phone up to her ear.

She listened to what felt like a five-minute voice mail, then dropped her phone back into her purse.

"OK, we can start heading in now," she said, an excited smile on her face.

"So, are you going to tell me what you're smiling about?" Dave said, jabbing his finger into her side to tickle her.

"Well, she just offered Liz and I "The Seahorse Inn."

"What? Are you kidding? That's worth at least a couple million. How will you afford that?"

"Oh, she's not selling it to us. She's offering to *give* it to us. They already have all the money they need from their business, and they never had any kids. Liz and I were the closest to daughters they ever had."

Dave's jaw dropped.

"I know. I think I'm too excited and overwhelmed to even comprehend this right now. It looks like Liz and I have a lot to talk about."

* * *

Pick up Book 2 in the Cape May Series**, Christmas in Cape May,** to follow Margaret, Liz, Dave, and the rest of the bunch.

Follow me on **Facebook** at www.facebook.com/Claudia-VanceBooks

ABOUT THE AUTHOR

Claudia Vance is a writer of women's fiction and clean romance. She writes feel good reads that take you to places you'd like to visit with characters you'd want to get to know.

She lives with her boyfriend and 2 cats in a charming small town in New Jersey, not too far from the beautiful beach town of Cape May. She worked behind the scenes on tv shows and film sets for many years, and she's an avid gardener and nature lover.

Copyright © 2020 by Claudia Vance

All rights reserved.

No part of this book may be reproduced in any form or by any electronic or mechanical means, including information storage and retrieval systems, without written permission from the author, except for the use of brief quotations in a book review.

Book Cover design by Red Leaf Design

This is a work of fiction. Names, places, events, organizations, characters, and businesses are used in a fictitious manner or the product of the author's imagination.

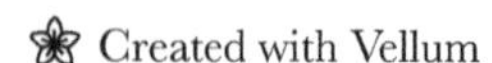